MW01675312

We were all coming to the same conclusion. I could tell because we all talked at the same time. Jess said, "They'll put you in jail" and Carly said, "They'll arrest you" and I said, "Jess will be the only one free to figure it all out."

Carly and I sat with our heads in our hands, and Jess went to the kitchen and rummaged around in the refrigerator.

Trouble *at the* Bagel Cafe

Also by Connie Miller Pease

Books:

Mrs. Covington's Sunday School Dropouts

Musicals:

Children's Musicals:

A Light At Christmas

Come, Messiah!

Full Length Musicals:

Whither

Found

Just One

Sheet Music:

Here Comes April Rain

I Hope To Love You

I Was Always There

In My Dreams

Just One

Softly Now He Comes

The Gift God Gave You

Find the author at www.myfiresidechat.com

Trouble at the Bagel Cafe

No Matter What You Do, You're Screwed

Connie Miller Pease

On the Dock Publishing

Author's Note: This novel is a work of fiction. Names, characters, places, and incidents are either products of the author's imagination or used fictitiously. All characters are fictional, and any similarity to people living or dead is purely coincidental.

Printed in the United States of America

Cover and Interior Design: Ghislain Viau

To Anna, Mary, Sarah Kate, and Ben who listened to my homemade stories throughout childhood. What was the squirrel's name—Ringtale? And remember Mallory who said there was trouble when there wasn't any trouble?

I hope you never outgrow the satisfaction of a good story, read, written, or lived.

To Abby, Sarah, Kathryn, Jamie, Emily, and Beth. You're in a cozy study stacked with old books and music. Sip some cherry cola and listen to your quirky aunt spin a tale.

Soli Deo Gloria

1

I didn't set out to have my life be a cautionary tale. When I was young, lying on my back on the dock, oblivious of the unforgiving slats of wood, amazed at the depth of blue the sky could offer; I dreamed of a comfortable sort of life in which sorrow would be barely noticeable and happiness would be as dependable as sunshine in July. I didn't know then that happiness and ease aren't necessarily interdependent.

August 8th following my graduation from high school was the last carefree day of my life. That was the day that I had off work at the flower shop where I had been lucky enough to find a part-time summer job and had gone to the beach with my friends, Carly and Jess. We went under the guise of relaxation. Actually, we were going to try for a tan—oh, I know what you're thinking, but we weren't thinking that. As

I was saying, we were going to try for a tan that would make it look like we were outdoorsy types; that, and to figure out what Carly should wear on her first date with Alden. I know. Right? ALDEN. His phone call had taken her so much by surprise she had choked on a grape she had been eating when she'd answered the phone, and hadn't been able to say much of anything other than yes during the entire minute and a half of their conversation. According to Carly it was both the longest and shortest minute and a half of her life. Alden was a guy from school who was so far beyond what any of us had every dreamed of dating, that the three of us had nearly asphyxiated ourselves during our breathless discussions while helping Carly choose what to wear.

Later that afternoon as I was smearing aloe vera gel all over my sufficiently cooked self, it occurred to me that while Carly would be out with Mr. Amazing, Jessica and I would be free to vicariously enjoy the evening if we were careful to stay out of their line of sight. I called Jess who immediately agreed. I guess that goes without saying. Jess is a like cheesy Christmas movie wrapped in fourth of July fireworks.

I swung by Jess's house at 6:30, and we were parked near Carly's house and out of my car in time for Alden to pick her up at 6:45 in his black Jeep.

We were nearly exposed when we giggled so loudly at Carly tripping as she got into the Jeep (Alden caught her before she fell) that her neighbor, Mr. Sullberger, came out and shooed us away from our hiding place behind his hedge.

The problem was that it was one of those fits of laughter that won't go away by will power alone. We could barely see clearly enough to get back to my beat-up Nissan and were beginning to get those stomachaches that come with over-exertion. You have to understand, by myself I'm perfectly normal, but Jess influences the air around her like a bottle of Coke that just swallowed a Mento. By the time we'd gotten to the movie, the show had started, and in the darkened theater we wouldn't be able to make out one couple from another. Rather than sit through the movie for the third time (we'd all gone together when it opened and then again a few days later to a matinee), we decided to wait it out at the little cafe across the street.

That was a mistake.

We had been sipping cherry colas for about thirty minutes or so and were waxing eloquent with imaginary tales of Carly and Alden's courtship, marriage, and six children when Jess got up to go to the bathroom. It was understandable. The glass in front of her was her third.

I was tapping out a counter rhythm to the latest platinum single when—crash! A couple of chairs were knocked over and three people at the table to my left hit the floor. What in the world? I caught the reflection of something in the window to my right, and a scuffle sounded from behind the counter. I hit my elbow on the booth as I hunched down and turned toward the commotion behind me where I saw a man in a hoodie grab money the cashier handed over. The cafe grew real quiet in a matter of seconds, though anyone with normal hearing should've been able to hear my heart thumping double time. One obnoxious lady screamed outright as a loud sound echoed through the room and she slumped over. I tried to look toward the bathrooms for Jess, but by that time the whole room was spinning, and I couldn't tell where to look. The man beat it out of that place like lightening, someone called the police, and the few of us who hadn't torn out of the emergency exit to the safety of home sat at the station for the rest of the night taking turns telling the policemen what we saw.

Jess hyperventilated only a couple of times after that night, and that was just her reaction to hearing about it. If she'd been sitting with me, she'd probably still be muttering incoherently in a white room somewhere. As it was, she was questioned the shortest amount of time of anyone there because she hadn't seen a thing.

Fortunately for her, The Bagel Cafe had recently renovated their bathrooms. Jess had been in there the whole time because she hadn't been able to figure out how to work the new sink faucets. They were motion-sensored, a big deal in our backward Midwest town, but that wasn't the only delay. The cafe had recently blown a wad of cash on those hand dryers that make your skin look like you're flying through space at warp speed. By the time Jess was sufficiently amazed and entertained, the whole thing was over.

We never did get to watch Alden take Carly home or see if he touched her back or brushed her hand with his or outright kissed her.

He must have, though, because after that night Jess and I saw so little of Carly, it was like she'd never existed. Oh, every once in awhile, I'd maybe catch a glimpse of her down the block or out in a boat on the lake, but I could only wave. You need to be within shouting distance to have a conversation.

2

"Ahem."

I looked up from my desk. It was Melissa, the high school girl I had hired to help me three days a week after school.

I laid aside an order form I was filling out for the flower shop. That's right. After getting in one year at college, I bought the place, ran it on a shoestring for a month, did the flowers for the biggest wedding this town had ever seen—Mr. Huesner's daughter, Tutti, was marrying the new high school gym teacher—and boom! Business took off like an ostrich feather on a fast bird. That lasted for, I'd say another couple of months, then business went back down to what people call stable and I call manageable. Big business might mean big money, but it also can mean big headaches. I've never been interested in big, preferring safe and easy to handle instead.

Actually, I was amazed that I owned the shop at all. I'd always been a rather average student and, after getting as far as an incomplete college degree, had come back home because I couldn't afford to do anything else. I got back my job at the flower shop easily enough. The owner, Trudy Tilden, had always liked me for some reason, despite my friends dropping by to say hello from time to time. She was what people used to call a spinster, then after a number of variations on a theme, referred to as an entrepreneur. Whatever it was that she was, she'd hacked out her living selling flowers for as long as this town could remember. Not long after I'd started working for her again, one day out of the blue she looked up from straightening the office, deliberately placed some mail in the top drawer of the desk, and asked if I wanted to buy the place. Just like that! Can you believe it?

I, of course, couldn't afford it, but a loan from the bank made the dream I hadn't had come true, and here I was. I didn't have to think about much because everything happened really fast. The shop was already stocked, of course. The place even came with a delivery driver and truck. Francis, the driver, knew every route there was to know within sixty miles, and he hadn't messed up an order in all the time I knew him. All I had to do was sign some papers and get the keys from Trudy.

Melissa's neck was becoming blotchy and she was alternately biting her upper and lower lip and various parts of the inside of her mouth.

"Just tell me, Mel. Is Mrs. Baxtrom not happy with her bouquet again this week?"

I was taught that if you can't say something nice about someone it's best to keep your mouth shut. Sometimes that's true, but not always. Otherwise, how can you warn a friend about an ax murderer, for instance? However, sometimes you can work it into conversation in such a way that you don't say something bad about a person and still get your point across. Persnickety is a word that means overly particular. I just thought I'd mention that at this point.

Mrs. Baxtrom's late husband had put in a standing order, charged to his estate, for a weekly bouquet to be delivered to his wife upon his death. Everyone thought it was the nicest thing. I thought he probably did it so she'd feel too guilty to ever be romantically involved with another man, but that's just me.

"No, no, it isn't Mrs. Baxtrom. It's . . ."

Melissa whispered the next part and I couldn't hear it.

"You'll have to say it out loud, Mel. Remember," I said pointing to my left ear, "the shootout at The Bagel Cafe left me with a souvenir."

I snorted a laugh. The hearing loss I'd been left with that summer night hadn't deterred me from much and I'd found it better to laugh about it than to complain. Usually.

Melissa leaned in.

"It's the police. Two!" she said, as if two policemen meant something that I should understand.

I let out a long sigh.

"It's okay," I replied, looking at the desk clock. "You know what? It's almost closing time. Why don't you just call 'er a day and lock up? I'll take care of the cash register."

I didn't need to say it twice. Melissa was a nice girl, but like most teenagers, she was more interested in the paycheck than the job itself.

"Send the two officers on back on your way out!" I called to her.

She had already grabbed her jacket and mini backpack and had her sights set on her bike chained to the post outside.

"Miss Calico?" Noah Berkl said as he knocked on the door frame of the back room otherwise known as the break room otherwise known as my office.

"I don't need your formalities, Noah."

I motioned for him and his friend to sit in the couple of chairs at the break table located on the other side of the door. They picked up the chairs and set them down in front of my desk instead.

"I see you've brought a friend this time," I remarked, barely escaping choking on my saliva.

I couldn't help it. The guy with Noah was the most gorgeous man I'd ever laid eyes on bar none.

"Kent Damon, FBI," he said as he half stood and offered his hand.

I shook it, thinking it would no doubt be the only time I would touch the hand or any other part of this fellow and that I should take advantage of it while the opportunity presented itself.

Kent leaned back in his chair and crossed his leg the way a man does; not the way a woman would; no, I could tell Kent would never do that. Noah might, but he didn't today. Today he leaned forward with his forearms on my desk and gave me a look that said, 'I'm sorry as I can be, but we have to go over this again.'

"Aaand," I thought, watching him, "he's going to say it: 3, 2 . . ."

Okay, wait. I'm stopping at 3, 2, 1 1/2 . . . because you're going to know my name now and it needs an explanation. I've always hated my name, but somewhere in my mother's sub-conscious, she wanted us all to be important; and the word "patrician", which means nobleman or aristocrat, was the best she could come up with—hence, my name is Patricia, since naming me Patrician would have been oh so slightly over-the-top. And while everyone else my age had cool names, I was given the name of someone who could be my grandmother. We all have our burdens to bear. Back to my story. 2, 1.

"I'm sorry, Patty, but we have to go over the evening of August 8th one more time."

"Would that be one more time as in the last one more time or the time before that?" I asked as I got up and pulled a cherry cola from the mini fridge.

"Want one?" I asked the men.

Noah shook his head and Kent just studied me. I popped the tab, took a sip, and returned to my chair.

Kent pulled out a folder and paged through it, hesitating at a few places—rereading, then closed it.

"So you heard a shot the evening of August 8th," he stated.

"Everyone heard a gunshot," I replied.

"And then you saw someone fall to the floor."

I nodded my head slowly and said slower still, "Every. One. Saw. Someone. Killed."

The two men looked at me silently. I looked back at them while our collective silence took up more space than my little office had room for.

Noah was the first to knuckle under. Of course. He cleared his throat.

"Actually, not everyone," he said.

"What do you mean 'not everyone'?"

"According to the record, you're the only person who claims someone was shot. No one else," Kent replied with an edge to his voice. "No body was found. Your statement conflicts with the others. You need to come with us for questioning."

He stood. I remained seated. I took a sip of cola, but inside I was feeling the beginnings of an explosion.

"I have been down for questioning oh, how many times, would you say, Noah?" I began quietly. "I am tired of questioning. Just because I happened to be in a cafe on the wrong night more than, I repeat—*more*—than a year ago, am I to be hounded multiple times after that because of it?"

I let them both have it now.

"You know, instead of asking the same questions over and over and *over* again to the same person who, by the way, can't hear out of her left ear for the rest of her life because she was in that cafe, why don't you look around for, oh, I don't know, the thief, maybe; the trigger guy maybe?! That's your *job* you, you, you stupid wunderkinds!"

Okay, I've never been much one for name-calling. It was the best I could come up with in my state. I don't know what to tell you about what that particular state was. It wasn't like hysteria. I've been there. It wasn't that. It was more like an anxiety anger mix with a dash of grumpiness thrown in.

Kent looked at Noah as if inquiring whether I was actually like whatever it was he was wondering I was like, or if it was a put on. A corner of Kent's mouth tugged up and he nodded.

* *

Three hours later, I put a pot of double strength coffee on to perk, slipped into my rattiest pair of sweats—they had passed the threadbare stage years before—and deadbolted the door of my apartment.

I slumped onto the couch and clicked on the TV in one move. I'd gotten the couch free from someone who'd posted a picture of it on Craigslist. The most that could be said of it was that it blended in. It would've blended into any surroundings it found itself in. It was one chameleon of a couch. It suited me perfectly.

I turned the TV volume up a couple decibels as I sorted through the day's mail.

The only way I knew I was staring into space instead of sorting through the assortment of letters in my hand was the sound of pounding on my door. I recognized it immediately and jumped up to let Jess in.

Jessica had never left town after that night at the Bagel Cafe. Instead, she'd canceled her plans to go to a university half way across the country and stayed at home, attending the local community college. She was marking time taking college classes part time and making annoying sales calls remotely for a spa in Arizona. But mainly she was waiting for a guy named Bobby whom she'd fallen for big time to fall as deeply as she had. I kind of wondered if she hadn't introduced us yet because seeing me would make her seem more ordinary to him. Jess's college babe presence would probably take a hit if I was around. Plus, it would be hard to find a convenient time to introduce us to each other since they'd already broken up and made up twice, and allowances for loss and recovery weeks had to be made.

She looked at the couch where I'd dropped the mail in a hodgepodge and pushed past me to pick it up.

First, she picked up the remote and muted the sound, pointing the thing at the TV as though she was a CEO and the TV was an eager intern awaiting orders. She raised her eyebrows as she shuffled through my mail like a card shark and found what she was looking for, holding up an unremarkable white envelope.

"How many is this now?"

"More than twelve," I said, not wanting to do the math and trying to make my voice sound nonchalant.

Jess handed me the letter and went to my refrigerator. Food was to her what Xanax was to the rest of the anxious public.

"When are you going to grow up?" she asked, slamming her hand on the nearby counter. A slight smile crossed my lips as I thought of the pack of cherry cola sitting on the refrigerator's second shelf. Since that night at the Bagel Cafe, I'd offered to buy her a cherry cola whenever we went somewhere. She hadn't touched it since then, even though she was in the restroom and missed the whole robbery murder thing. So I made it a policy to keep it stocked at all times. What can I say? I thought it was funny.

"When are *you*?" I asked, walking past her to the coffeepot.

I emptied the pot into two oversized mugs and handed one to her. She rummaged around for some of that mint stuff you put on ice cream when you're feeling like a lady of leisure, poured a third of the bottle into her coffee and topped it with whipped cream. Jess had issues.

"So I heard through the grapevine that there were two cops at the store today."

"The Flower Cart," I corrected her.

Way back when Trudy Tilden had made the leap from her flower cart to a storefront, she hadn't been able to think of anything clever to name the place; so she'd just taken the umbrella canvas off her cart, tacked it on the awning of the store, kept the name of her business, and saved the money it would have taken for an actual sign. I knew it was lame, but by the time I took over it was the only name everyone would recognize. I tried to pretend it was a matter of pride. It was, but not in the manner I tried to pretend.

Jess wasn't having any of my false offense and rolled her eyes the way she did when I pretended I really didn't want the last piece of pizza.

"Well?" she asked.

"Same thing."

"It's always the same thing, Patty."

"And it was again," I said with more irritation than was necessary.

I picked up the white envelope and opened it.

"Only this time Noah brought a hunky guy named Kent. Kent Damon."

My one word description got enough of Jess's attention that she momentarily stopped slurping her coffee.

"Go on," she said, some of the ol' Jessica sparkle we all knew and loved coming into her eyes.

I leaned back into the couch. I'd learned it's best to be comfortable during an inquisition.

"He," my face felt a little warm, "He was probably 6 feet, maybe 6'2", dark hair . . ."

"Dark like coal black or dark like dark brown or was it like tree bark after rain?"

"You know, Jess, you tend to sound like an attorney for the prosecution when you do this."

"Do what? I'm just curious. Now go."

I sighed. "Maybe tree bark after rain?"

Jess nodded and made a rolling motion with her hand indicating I should continue.

"He had a strong jaw . . ."

"Like a bulldog or like a Greek god?"

"A Greek god. He had a strong handshake . . ."

Jess grabbed my face and looked in my eyes.

"You shook his hand?"

Her hands went up and down with my nod. I pulled them down.

"What did it feel like? Was it . . ."

"It was firm, okay?!"

Jess pulled back.

"You don't have to get testy. Please? Just a little more?"

After a blow by blow description of his physique, Jess wanted to know what his voice was like, whether I caught a whiff of his breath, and, if so, was it minty. I did my best, but, honestly, by this time, I was getting a little tired. Caffeine always did that to me: crashed me right into the next day.

"I'm tired, Jess. I need to call it a day," I said, starting to my bedroom to put on my pajamas.

Okay, I admit some people wouldn't call them pajamas. They wouldn't call them anything because they'd be too busy gasping or tittering. See, Jess, meaning well as usual, had picked them up on clearance for me as a sleepover surprise our junior year in high school. They were snuggly soft. They were also striped, but not in a way that made me look like a walking candy cane, which would have been at least tolerable. The stripes were horizontal. I looked like I gained thirty pounds just by putting them on. And they weren't red and white, but black and white, much like prison uniforms of yesteryear, which I suspect was the reason for the probably ninety-eight percent markdown. Oh who's kidding who? Of *course* it was the reason she got such a good deal. The sales lady probably would have *paid* her to take them if Jess had known anything about negotiating. They were also the most comfortable things you can imagine.

"Come back here."

"Really. I'm telling you the truth. You can crash on my couch if you want."

Jess grabbed the remote and turned up the volume. From my bedroom, I could hear her channel surfing, finally landing on a show I loved and she knew I loved.

She slid over, making room for me on the couch the minute my toe was on the threshold of my bedroom. By the time I got to the couch she was holding up the envelope like a school teacher with an unfinished assignment.

I grabbed it from her and pulled out the familiar lined paper.

"Out loud, please," she said.

"Dear Ms. Calico," I read, sighing, "Talk is cheap. It's also a way to disappear. I'm watching you."

"That's it?"

I shoved the letter over to her and her lips moved as she reread the words.

"Disappear?"

I ran my hand through my hair.

"If I had a clue about what I wasn't supposed to say, it would help."

"You have no idea what this letter says you might say?" She raised her eyebrows.

I shrugged. First of all who would I say anything to if I had something to say? The letter-writer could live one door down or half-way across the country. I had no idea who it was. Secondly, I really don't like trouble, including being the cause of it. Keeping your mouth shut and your head down wasn't the worst thing anyone could do. It's probably how half the population of the world survives depending on their neighborhood or government. I avoided her eyes and tried to watch the show that I loved.

"Look," Jess said, "who knows where Carly even is now? For all we know she's in Paris studying her art. It'll be going on a year and a half before long. I lost track of her the summer she started dating Alden."

Jess squinted her eyes. "Do you think she went to the same college as he did? I mean weirder couples have coupled. Like—oh what's the name of the one actress who's in everything—you know the one, and, um, that guy who's a financier and was involved with the one singer who dresses like a slut but acts all offended if anyone mentions it, but then left her for—oh you know who I'm talking about."

She was hitting my arm by now in her effort to recall names that most people other than me would remember.

"Though honestly, Carly should've at least given us a heads up. If she did end up at the same university as Alden, no one would've celebrated with her like us. It still seems pretty ungrateful of her to just go her merry way without even a decent goodbye. Whoever this is," she concluded, holding up the letter, "is just trying to scare you. They probably don't even know what Carly looks like."

The feeling in the pit of my stomach every time one of these letters came in the mail was growing from the size of a sunflower seed to the size of an avocado pit. I bit my thumbnail and sighed. I got up, walked over to the cupboard where I kept my pizza pan, took it out, letting it crash on the floor for good measure, and pulled out the box that I kept behind it. Opening it up, I sorted through some of the letters and brought one over to Jess, dropping it in her lap.

"Oh," she said quietly as she looked at the picture of Carly that had been tucked into the letter. The picture looked like it was taken the summer of—let's just call it 'the incident'.

For the next ten or fifteen minutes I watched my show as every so often Jess turned to me and opened her mouth to say something, then shut it again. I understood. I had been there a thousand times, myself.

See, not even a month after the craziness at the Bagel Cafe, I left for college. I'd moved into my tiny little dorm room with the weirdest roommate you'd ever hope to meet and settled down for what I thought would be four years of books, boring lectures, and buff college boys. I had adjusted to my roomie's taste for weird music and weirder hours, and she had adjusted to what she must have presumed to be my exotic small town habits of going to bed by midnight and waking up on time for class.

I got that first letter the third week of September. It was the longest of the trail of letters that came without regard for a schedule except that one arrived sometime in every month afterward. It said that the writer knew who I was and where I lived. It said the writer knew what happened at the Bagel Cafe that night. And it said if I told anyone what I really saw, something awful would happen to my sweet little friend Carly. All I had to do was to keep my mouth shut and life would be peachy. Except it wasn't peachy at all. Getting a letter every month reminding you of a night you would rather forget in the first place made you remember it in all its glaring detail even more.

Jess knew this much. What she didn't know was what I saw, because I couldn't bring myself to tell her. And that was that I saw Alden's Jeep pull away from the cafe just after the thief sprinted out the door.

3

That wasn't the only thing I saw, but thinking about the rest of it made me loopier than a roller coaster, so I mostly tried to ignore it; except one piece of mail every month of the year for over a year made that impossible. Who does that? Who sends mail to a stranger besides advertisers? What kind of twisted thinking prompts such an action and what kind of unyielding will continues it? It was a problem, but I didn't know what to do about it.

See, besides being friends, we were kind of like Carly's life jacket and rocking chair rolled into one. She didn't have any brothers or sisters—which I thought was pretty great. After all, it gave her first dibs on everything. What wasn't to love? She didn't see it that way, though. I kind of saw where she was coming from because it wasn't just the whole only child thing. Her parents didn't care much for their parents. So she didn't really know her cousins and all the rest of the people who made up her family tree; which, according to Carly, was more like a sickly thing pestered by emerald ash borers than the strong oak on the pictures where you fill in the little lines with names and dates. After her folks had been killed in a drunk driving accident just before high school graduation, Jess and I filled in the gap that was left. We weren't that great at it, but Carly didn't have anybody else. She didn't even have the satisfaction of vindication because the drunk driver disappeared into the netherworld of the justice system.

The phrase between a rock and a hard place means that no matter what you do you're screwed. But that was where I'd been for over a year. If I tried to look up Carly, it might put her in danger, because according to the letters it was all over for her if I told the police. Plus I wasn't convinced the whole department wouldn't just turn it back on me and claim I was behind it. They said I was the only one who reported a gunshot. Their unwanted attention made me wonder if they actually thought I said that to misdirect them or something. And another thing I wasn't happy I'd even thought, but I did: what if Carly was in on it? What if, for some reasons unknown to us, her best friends, she'd gone sour? If I said something to Jess, she'd end up eating the entire contents of my refrigerator, her refrigerator, and her crush's refrigerator (in the event he ever actually invited her to his house) and keep it up until sometime in the next decade, losing both him and the decade in the process.

I leaned forward, elbows on my knees, and rested my forehead in my hands. I rubbed it while I was trying to make up my mind. I could feel the warmth from Jess's hand hovering over my back like she wasn't sure whether to pat me or leave me alone.

I took the easiest choice for me and the hardest one for Jess. After all, a year and then some is a long time and something needed to change. Telling Jess was a surefire way to cause the earth to move somewhere in the world. Besides, who needs a boyfriend?

I sat up, shook off the tension with a shoulder shimmy, and put my hands on Jess's shoulders. Her eyes got real big, like she couldn't make them big enough to take everything in.

"You have to promise not to tell another soul, not even Bobby buff , what I'm going to tell you."

Jess crossed her heart, spit on her fingers, and wiped them on my pajama sleeve.

"Okay. Okay, I can do this," I said aloud to myself.

I leaned back on the couch and Jess leaned forward, studying my face.

"That night,"

"Yes?"

"When you left the table, I saw a reflection of a guy in the window, maybe another guy—I don't know—and the guy who was robbing the place. Then he or someone with him pointed to me and that was when they shot the lady."

"Why would they point to you?"

"How would I know?!" I yelled.

I cleared my throat.

"Sorry. The whole thing makes me irritable."

Jess nodded uncertainly.

"Did you see his face?"

"I," I shook my head, "I can't be sure. Anyway, I heard some noises, and that's when I turned and saw the cashier shove the money at the guy."

"And that's when he shot that poor lady?"

"I don't know who shot her. I thought one of them shot her."

Jess looked at me and squinted.

"The shot came from right beside me. It was, I swear, right next to me. I never saw a gun, though," I added as if that would make things more morally acceptable.

I was against guns. Absolutely. I had a sign on the door of The Flower Cart that said so. Jess, on the other hand, thought that if everyone had a gun the world would be a safer place. She kept one stashed in an oatmeal box in her cupboard and I continued to meditate on world peace. It wasn't the first reason we thought the other was just a little bit crazy and it wouldn't be the last.

Jess got up and went to the refrigerator. Seeing the pack of cherry cola, she slammed it shut, pulled a stale donut from a box on the counter, and started nibbling at it while she paced back and forth in my living room.

Though I was on my own, all I could afford was a small apartment in one of the sketchiest parts of town. I got dizzy looking at her because pacing in a room that size is more like twirling every few steps.

"Sit. You're making me dizzy," I said.

Jess finally shrugged her shoulders.

"So more than one person was in on it. So what? Why didn't you tell the police?"

"I *did* tell the police. The first night of questioning at the police station I told them there had to be more than one person. It's got to be right there in the files."

"Well okay then. Everything's out in the open, right?" Jess said with relief in her voice.

"Except at subsequent questioning, they look at me like I'm making something up, like I'm adding to my original statement. Or subtracting. I don't know. They say I didn't tell them about a third person that first night and then they look at me like I'm contradicting myself. And today they told me I'm contradicting other witnesses."

"But if you told them the second time . . ."

"And third. Yea. And every time I tell them they look at me like I'm trying to pull a fast one, and they study the original statement maybe or whatever papers they have in front of them, and then they write something down."

"What do they write down?"

"How should I know! I finally just gave up. Now I go in there and I tell them about you and me being in there for thirty minutes . . ."

"Only thirty? It felt like longer."

"Maybe. I don't know. We weren't exactly keeping track of time. And I tell them about the lady screaming and the sound of a gun going off and seeing the guy run out the door with the cash."

"Well name names, Patty. Give them a name of who you think was in on it. That ought to get their attention."

I nodded my head. It wasn't like I hadn't been down that road already. Going down it I felt more and more like a highway worker picking up trash and looking for every single piece of litter there was.

"Think, Jess. Think who was in there that night."

I waited for her to think it over. She scratched her head, then closed her eyes and put her fingers to her temples. She finally opened them and stared into space, kind of like I'd been doing for the past year and a half.

"Huh."

"Yea," I replied.

"I'm probably not remembering right, Patty. There had to be someone there who . . ." her voice drifted into thin air.

"Someone who we knew?" I picked up her train of thought, "Surely someone who we knew in a town small enough for you to know at least five people every single place you go? I've gone over and over it in my head. I can't think of a single person in the cafe that night whose name I knew. Besides, it wasn't like we were paying attention to the customers what with marrying Carly off to Alden and all. And maybe, Jess," I continued, "Maybe I could think up someone.

I mean it's been long enough that if I imagine it often enough I can imagine someone I know having been there. Then comes this question. Which person are you going to point your finger at and ruin their life thinking your imagination just might be real? Which person who we've known all our lives, who still lives here and buys their groceries at Lundborg's Grocery Mart and cheers for the high school football team on Friday nights and walks down the streets of this town was in on it?"

Jess's cell buzzed and from the look on her face I could tell it was some mushy text from Bobby. They must be recovering nicely from their second break-up.

"He says he has a tulip looking for two lips." She shook her head, smiling. "Clever, huh?"

Oh my word.

"Go," I said, keeping my other thoughts to myself.

Jess got up and carried her coffee mug to the sink.

"We're not finished with this. I'll poke my head into your office tomorrow. Maybe hunky Kent will stop by your little flower store . . ."

"The Flower Cart,"

". . . again and I can see him for myself," said Jess on her way out the door.

The sound of the door closing tight and Jess's quick steps down the hall disappeared.

"And I've never told them about Alden's Jeep," I mumbled as I clicked off the TV and deadbolted the door.

4

Mrs. Baxtrom was standing in front of the counter. She was a sweet old thing. Her face had those soft wrinkles that some women get with age; not the kind that are sharply creased, but the kind that take on more of a gently folded quality. Her voice was lower than it should have been, but age and a long smoking habit had done a job on it.

That voice had, bit by bit, become a permanent fixture in The Flower Cart. I even had a dream once in which I heard it in the background, like the voice of a narrator reporting the events of whatever catastrophe my brain was dreaming up at the time. Besides receiving the flowers Mr. Baxtrom had arranged to be sent to her every week upon his death, by virtue of being treasurer of the local garden club, she believed herself to be an expert on everything bold enough to grow out of the ground.

"Did you hear me, Patty?" she said in that way she had that made you wish you could show her the door.

Although she was a sweet old thing, she could get on your nerves sometimes.

"Yes, Ma'am," I held up the special request she'd written out for flowers for the garden club meeting—the same one she wrote out every time she ordered and the same one she told me as she handed me the request. "Two dozen roses: six red, six white, six pink, six yellow."

Mrs. Baxtrom nodded her head slightly and cocked it to one side. The clock on the counter ticked loudly proclaiming to the world it was noon and all reasonable people should be eating lunch. She was waiting for me to finish, to tell her where I was supposed to send them. I already knew where they needed to be delivered because she had just told me and because it was written underneath the request, but she seemed to think that I wouldn't know what she said unless I repeated it back to her. It was one of those times I thought to myself that perhaps Mr. Baxtrom was fortunate in his demise. I immediately felt guilty.

She was just leaving when the entry door bell tinkled and Jess walked in.

"You got anything in that mini fridge back there?" she called as she passed the counter, "I'm on my lunch break and could eat an elephant."

"Bad day?" I asked, following her back.

I had all the orders except Mrs. Baxtrom's ready for Francis to haul to the van when he arrived and figured I had some down time coming. It wasn't like The Flower Cart was a bustling place of commerce.

"That Mrs. Baxtrom of yours doesn't like me," Jess said between mouthsful of King crab salad I'd bought at the deli on my way to work.

I pointed to the container and raised my eyebrows.

Jess jabbed another forkful in her mouth and looked back at me.

"What?"

I sighed. I wasn't that hungry anyway. Francis had been waiting for me when I opened and had given me an enormous Bear Claw he'd picked up at the gas station convenience store out on Highway 12. He and I had joked around while I opened the cash register and did a few mundane things, and he made us coffee and hauled fresh flowers to the display case. He'd admired the selections I'd ordered from the warehouse where I got most of my inventory and promised to be back for his deliveries after lunch.

"She purses her lips every time she sees me," Jess persisted.

"One, she's not *my* Mrs. Baxtrom. Two, maybe it's because every time she sees you, you're barging into this place like you own it."

"Well, it's not like *she* owns it, so what's her problemo, eh?"

Jess lapsed into pretend Spanish every once in awhile. It was all part of the Jessica mystique, one that Carly and I occasionally copied out of a sense of solidarity.

"So how was it with Bobby buff last night?"

We called him that because Jess's descriptions of him left no room for doubt about his muscle tone.

Jess waved the question away with my fork.

"Meh. I'm beginning to suspect he's dating me for my tutorial services."

"There are worse reasons to date someone, I suppose."

Jess furrowed her brow.

I added, "I thought he was older."

"Yea, there's that." She poked at the salad with her fork. "But age-wise he's still in the window of 'eligible'. I don't know. Maybe he just decided to bump up his academic resume, and sees me as a living, breathing handbook, a handy byproduct, a coadjutor."

She stuffed an oversized forkful into her mouth.

"Well look at you with the big words."

"It's an assignment," Jess replied, still chewing, "to work one vocab word into conversation per day this week." She swallowed. "I covered two days with that sentence, didn't I?"

I nodded supportively.

"But I'm serious, Patty. A year ago I took the college classes he's taking now and lately it's all homework and no, no…"

Her voice drifted off in a fuzzy world of not quite right adjectival nouns that wished with all their might they were verbs but never would be that active.

"All I want is the dream, you know?"

Oh, I knew. Jess's dream wasn't every girl's dream, but it was hers and included a man of her dreams rescuing her from every bad thing and romanticizing her like a poet.

"Maybe he's just distracted with coursework. Maybe he's looking to you to do the rescuing so he can rescue you later."

Jess screwed her mouth to one side.

"He's pretty amazing. He's hot, and I mean smokin'. I'm sure I'm lucky to have him."

Jess was on a roll trying to convince herself that the most recent break-up make-up was the right thing to do.

She tired of it pretty quickly, though, because in the next breath she said, "You and I didn't finish our conversation. So I was thinking, all we have to do is find out who was there that night."

Jess grabbed a pen lying on my desk, snatched a piece of paper from the wastebasket, and looked up expectantly.

"I've got nothing," I reminded her, picking up a paper clip and playing with it as we talked.

"Aw."

She reached for the paperclip, kissed it to the pen, and handed it back to me.

That was Jess for you. The romantic in her might take a short break, but it could revive as fast as a plant in the rain.

See, I know that if you dream about paperclips, it means you need to hold certain aspects of your life together (at this point I should have been dreaming about a whole box of them). And, while it's true that in World War II paperclips were used as a symbol of resistance (that is, until the Germans figured it out and made wearing a paperclip a criminal offense which was seriously stupid, if you ask me), and that back in the 40's and 50's there was a secret program named Operation Paperclip having to do with paperclipping Germans onto American society, Jess knew differently. When I was in the third grade, Kirk Kendall tried to flirt with me by giving me two of his. They were pink. Apparently, I didn't make goo-goo eyes at him well enough, and the next day he gave three green ones to a girl named Sophia. Anyway, to this day paperclips make me think of unsung love. Sad, I know. Jess thought it was romantic. What a pitiful pair we are.

"Okay then. Let's go back there. We can have supper there after work, huh?"

As soon as she had made the suggestion, Jess started tapping my pen on my desk at a frenetic pace. We hadn't been back to the Bagel Cafe since that night nearly fifteen months ago. I had no problem with going back, especially since this was a small town, and not going there had basically limited our out-to-eat dining experiences to the Subway, Mac's Truck Stop, Nonni's Steak House, or driving ten miles to the next town. Jess, on the other hand, had steadfastly refused to go there ever again. It was all she could do to go to the movie theater across the street; and that was only for amazing movies that, if she had to wait to come out on a subscription-based service, would add too much angst to her already high levels of anxiety.

I shrugged, but my stomach was doing happy little flutter kicks. I wasn't in the habit of eating out alone, so Jess's avoidance had kept me from the best burger basket in town. If we went there and looked around the place again, maybe it would jog a memory or two. It would be great if we could identify someone who had been there and maybe figure out something to do so the letters would stop coming every month.

Jess ran her finger around the inside of the deli carton, dropped it into the wastebasket, and, licking her finger, peeked into the refrigerator again, pulling a frozen M & M cookie out of the mini freezer compartment. Taking a bite, she looked at her watch, inhaled a little too deeply, and immediately started choking up a storm.

Francis came for the afternoon's deliveries, I hurried to fix the remaining one, the one Mrs. Baxtrom had ordered just before Jess walked in, and didn't see her leave. She probably squealed her tires on the way out, because Francis came back on the dot of 1:00 every day and no one in this town ever heard of an hour-long lunch break.

* *

It was closing time, and I was anxious to meet Jess for supper and reconnaissance at the Bagel Cafe. Actually, I was hoping I could intercept her before she reached the door of the place at which time I was fully convinced she would change her mind and suggest we go across the street and take in a movie instead.

Melissa was sweeping the floor and I was comparing prices from the big city wholesale warehouse catalogue to the prices on an invoice, when Francis came in. He'd forgotten something and walked over to the small counter that held the coffee pot and a few other things to pick up whatever it was. He rummaged around and then turned, leaning against the counter.

Shaking his head, he said, "I think some days I'd forget my head if it wadn't screwed on, Patty."

"What'd you forget?" I laughed as I stacked the papers and put them in my desk.

"Oh, nothing important to you or me," he replied, patting his pocket where he must've slipped the missing item. "My daughter, though—dis little trinket means something to her. I must've dropped it dis morning when I was making coffee."

"You should bring her in sometime. I've only seen her from a truck window."

"Oh she a little monkey. I bring her in here an' she run aroun' an' knock three things over before you can say hello."

"You're being modest, Francis. I saw her name on the list of children from Central Elementary who received the good citizenship award last month. It was in the local paper."

Francis beamed while I cashed out the register and locked it.

"We were so proud, Patty. My wife sent a million copies to relatives."

He picked things up and put them down again, puttering around as he continued chatting about Jose who lived in Texas, Marita and her family who were in New Mexico, and a myriad of other colorful souls still living in his hometown south of the border.

Francis wasn't known for being all business. He had the type of temperament that made you feel like you were somewhere in Mexico with the sun high in the sky and people around you had their sombreros pulled half way down their faces and were breathing slowly. No. There was no hurry in Francis's world. Melissa had already left by the time I was gathering my things to leave. Francis glanced around the office.

"You already found your daughter's trinket," I reminded him.

"Yes, yes," he agreed with another glance. "I might as well empty dis for you on my way out, Patty," he offered, stooping down to fasten the liner of wastebasket by my desk with a twisty tie.

I patted him on the back. It's hard to find good men like that, men who do more than they're paid to do. We walked out together, and I locked the doors while he headed for the dumpster.

I waved to him, and he waved back as I beat him out of the parking lot. I was in a hurry to meet Jess who would have expected me at least thirty minutes earlier.

That conversation with Francis had delayed me enough so that it was the end of the supper rush by the time I walked into the Bagel Cafe. Jess was sitting at the table where we had been the night of August 8th. A full water glass sat in front of her, untouched. Seeing her from the doorway, she looked like what a bystander would think she was—a bored patron waiting for a tardy companion—until I noticed her leg which was jiggling up and down like she was running the last ten yards of the Boston Marathon in a dead heat with her competition.

"Where have you *been*?!" she whisper shouted toward my right side as I slid into the booth across from her.

She knew which ear to favor, the other being dead an' all. That's what she called it: my dead ear. I didn't correct her. Deaf or dead, the result was the same.

"I'm sorry, Jess. Francis stopped by and you know how he talks. It was all I could do to get here by now."

Mercifully for both of us, the waitress came to take our orders. I ordered the Bagel Burger Basket and a cherry cola.

If looks could kill I would have been down on the floor by the time the waitress turned to take Jess's order. After she left to place our orders, Jess shook her head.

"What?" I asked innocently.

"If you weren't my friend since second grade, I'd deck you here and now," Jess said.

"Breathe, Jess. Besides, I think this is good for you. I read once that if you immerse yourself in the thing you fear, pretty soon the regular fear doesn't seem so bad after all, kind of like learning to eat the Jello you're afraid of drowning in. Only they didn't say it that way. Immotion. Inpossion. No. Implosion. Yeah. They called it something like that."

"Well you're going to have an *ex*plosion on your hands if you don't stop with the cherry colas."

The waitress brought us our drinks just then. Sometimes life is like that. You think something should happen right at a certain time and, boom, it does.

"I like cherry cola," I said, and slurped from the straw, "and so do you."

I reached over and patted Jess's hand as I motioned for the waitress.

Jess poured some creamer into her coffee and eyed me warily.

"Yea. She'd like a cherry cola, too."

The waitress nodded as Jess gave me a sharp kick under the table. She didn't have time to rant, though, because just then someone of note walked into the cafe. I had my back to the door, but Jess caught sight of them immediately and automatically held up her spoon to take a quick glance at her reflection in the back of it. I turned to see who it was as our waitress brought Jess's cherry cola.

Noah Berkl and Kent Damon saw me and stopped by the table. Jess took a flirtatious sip from her straw without thinking.

"Nice night for supper out," Noah remarked. "I eat in with the wife mostly, but not tonight."

I nodded, "Our waitress said the fries are extra crispy tonight."

"I'm surprised to see you here, Patty," Noah continued.

"I can't imagine why," I said, swallowing as I sideways glanced at Kent.

Jess wasn't sideways glancing at all. She was full on staring and sipping her cherry cola like she was dehydrated.

"Last time we talked you said you hadn't been back here since the night of the robbery."

Kent looked at me with the kind of look that had all sorts of thoughts behind it. I just couldn't tell which thoughts those thoughts were.

I took a sip from my glass and looked back at him.

"I *haven't* been here since then," I answered. "But Jess and I had a free evening. We were talking earlier and decided we'd just stop by for old time's sake."

"What were you talking about?" asked Kent.

"What?"

"You said Jess and you were talking and it sounded to me like whatever it was that you were talking about prompted you to come here."

It appeared, regrettably, Kent's preferred manner of small talk leaned less toward chit chat and more toward interrogation. I couldn't think of a thing to say. I wasn't going to tell him that we were reconnoitering here to try to figure out some things about the crime on our own.

"Actually, Kent, is it?" Jess began, nudging my foot with hers.

Kent gave a barely perceptible nod.

"We were just reminiscing about the old days and thought it'd be fun to come back here. Having been college girls 'n all, we were kind of missing those old carefree days."

I thought I'd better say something before Jess wrote her address on a napkin. If Bobby buff needed proof he had messed up big time with his focus on homework earlier, he could soon get it.

"There aren't all that many places to eat out in this town," I said, "We finally got tired of Subway."

That was so not true, but I said it anyway.

Noah looked at his watch.

"Enjoy your dinner, ladies," he said as he started toward a booth near the back.

Kent looked at me for a split second longer, then followed him back.

Jess looked across the table at me and mouthed "WOW" in capital letters. I knew they were capital letters because she opened her mouth every possible inch when she mouthed the word.

"Told you," I said, low.

After all, even if he was quickly becoming someone it would be better for me to avoid since it seemed like he suspected me of some nefarious ploy (which, if he knew me at all he would know I was totally incapable of), there was no getting around the fact that God had given Kent an appearance of breathtaking proportions.

We went over the entire evening of August 8th in whispered tones. Our memories were pretty short on specifics.

"Wait. The lady you saw get shot? She was wearing cowboy boots with her skinny jeans tucked into them and some kind of loose, flowy blouse." Jess chewed on a french fry. "It was—hmm—floral—I think in the green family."

"Oh great. We can remember what a dead woman was wearing. That should be a big help," I said, sighing.

"But you said the police said whoever it was didn't shoot her," Jess said, tilting her head in a quizzical manner.

"Right."

I closed my eyes, trying to see back a year and a half.

"Her body was," I pointed, "there."

"The gun was," I swatted my hand to my left, "here.

"I. . . huh. . . I don't recall seeing it, but maybe it had become part of the background to me by that point. After all, it was a weird, weird night."

"Weird," Jess agreed, "She had been eating a fried egg and toast. And!"

In my peripheral vision I saw Noah look our direction and Kent's back stiffen.

"Jessicaaa," I cautioned.

"Oh. Right," she whispered back.

She dabbed at her mouth with her napkin.

"What?!" I whisper shouted.

"Well, I'm thinking that when we were discussing Carly and Alden's fifth child,"

"The one we named Nakita Mae," I inserted.

"Yes. That a fellow came in for a coffee to go."

"That is so interesting I'll lose sleep over it," I replied.

"A fellow who reminded me of Alden for some reason," she finished triumphantly.

I tapped my finger on the edge of the table. The waitress passed by and I motioned her for a refill of my cherry cola. She took both our glasses, and returned with two full ones, placing one in front of each of us. For a split second I thought Jess was going to cry.

"Well? Was it?"

"Was it what?"

"Was it Alden? I mean it couldn't have been because he was at the movie with Carly, right? But what if he slipped out? Maybe he slipped out, Jess."

Jess narrowed her eyes at me.

"Alden taking Carly to the movie was what started this whole stupid thing," she said slowly as though reminding me of a basic fact, like the alphabet. "Of *course* it wasn't Alden. He just reminded me of Alden, that's all."

"Are you sure?"

"Are you crazy?" she answered. "Yes, I'm sure. He was taller and older and had shorter hair. Plus he had a different look—oh I don't know—like he was similar but different."

"Ah ha. Similar, but different."

Jess sat back and folded her arms across her chest.

"I don't know what else to say. He reminded me, that's all. Why are you jumping on Alden all of a sudden? All he did was buy our friend some popcorn. I think. Do you think he bought her popcorn?"

"I'm sure he did," I said reassuringly.

"I . . . Jess, this is weird," I said, "but I thought I saw Alden's Jeep pull away when the guy ran out of here that night."

Jess leaned forward.

"No way."

"I'm just sayin'. I'm pretty sure it was his Jeep."

"And you're just now telling me this?"

"I keep thinking I'm wrong. That I saw it wrong."

"Carly would not do something like that."

"Who said anything about Carly?"

"She was with Alden," Jess answered.

"But would Alden?" I asked, saying out loud for the first time what I hadn't even dared to think for over a year.

"Mr. straight A, gorgeous, athletic, perfect guy?" Jess asked.

"Would Alden do something like that?" I persisted simply because maybe saying it would help me understand what I'd seen.

"But if Alden," Jess's voice went froggy.

Jess straightened, cleared her throat, and began again.

"If Alden did something horrible like this."

She stopped.

"No. I can't even match that with him. He was Mr. Amazing."

I nodded.

"I know."

"Patty. Is that why you never mentioned it? Because you didn't want to believe it?"

I slowly leaned my head left and right, wondering if what she asked was true. Then I shrugged.

"You didn't want to believe it just now either."

"You still hungry?" Jess asked with a suddenness that made me jump.

"C'mon, honey. Time for us to get out of here."

Clearly Jess's anxiety level was climbing to a place that would lead to loud belching and moaning. Getting her out of the restaurant was the loyal thing to do.

She needed to get home before her jitters took over completely. We walked out to where our cars were parked on the street and I started rummaging in my bag for my keys. I looked up and saw through the window that Kent was standing by the table, looking at us.

"Patty!"

Jess was shouting like it was the fifth time she'd said my name and was past peeved.

"I said do you want this?"

She was holding out a slip of paper.

"What is it?"

"I used the back of it when we were talking in your office earlier. I was going to throw it away, since it's from the wastebasket in your shop, but when I turned it over it looked like maybe it was something important."

I took the paper, folded it, and shoved it in my pocket.

It wasn't until I had a cup of coffee to settle my nerves and was changing into my pajamas that I remembered the paper. I pulled it out of the pocket of my jeans. On one side were Jess's doodling and notes. Written on the other side were names—names that seemed odd; not odd as in foreign, but odd as in . . . odd—and phone numbers, some abbreviations I didn't understand, a couple of addresses, and a small map.

5

I awoke in the middle of the night with an uneasy feeling; the kind of feeling that makes you think you've left something undone that needs to be done by the next day. Then I remembered the paper resting on my bedside table. I glanced over at it.

I'd examined the piece of paper that Jess had handed to me for nearly a quarter of an hour before I went to bed. What should I care about a piece of trash? There were a couple of things about it, though, that bothered me. First, it wasn't mine, and since it wasn't, how did it get in the wastebasket by my desk? Customers weren't allowed in the back room. The only other people who could have thrown it away would have been Melissa or maybe Francis. Melissa only did what I asked her to do, which didn't include anything to do with writing other than jotting something on those tiny cards inserted in the flower deliveries. She had nice handwriting and so she was my go-to girl for that when she was available which was three afternoons a week, or about nine hours of the forty-two the shop was open. The writing on the paper wasn't hers. I would've recognized it. I knew Francis could read instructions I gave him about deliveries, but I didn't know if he could write English—it was his second language after all. But he didn't strike me as someone who would have made an effort to learn beyond what was necessary, so that possibility was pretty much out. I thought for another minute. Yea, probably.

Then there was Noah and Kent's visit. It wasn't like I was a cleaning machine. That wastebasket wasn't emptied every day. In fact, it would've still had stuff in it if Francis hadn't offered to take it out to the trash. So it could've been something one of them tossed in there. All I recalled from their visit was talking, getting miffed, and, of course, a rapid heartbeat on first sight of Kent Damon. No one would ever accuse me of being highly observant. Did those names (and phone numbers and addresses and map and abbreviations) mean anything to their investigation of that night at the Bagel Cafe? I had decided I would hold on to the paper until I was certain it wasn't something that should interest me.

When I woke up in the middle of the night, though, that nagging feeling made me think that I had seen that handwriting before, and,for the life of me I couldn't think of where.

* *

The next day was Saturday. Saturdays were easy as far as The Flower Cart went. Trudy Tilden had trained the customers to expect service Monday through Friday only. That was when she had pushed her flower cart around town, and she didn't change her schedule just because she had a storefront. If someone had a Saturday night date or a Sunday afternoon anniversary, they had to plan ahead. It was as simple as that.

I had pity on them, though, because I was one of those that didn't exactly plan everything in advance; so I'd expanded The Flower Cart's hours to include from ten to noon on Saturdays.

I got up at 9:00, showered and dressed, grabbed the paper from my bedside and stuffed it into my purse, and was at the store by ten minutes to opening. Francis was waiting for me. His eyes were bloodshot. I felt a little sorry for him.

"Let me see about the deliveries, Francis," I said, hurriedly unlocking the door. "Hopefully there aren't so many that you can't get back to bed and sleep off that hangover," I called over my shoulder as I unlocked the cash register.

Francis followed me into my office and started the coffee while I dropped my purse into the bottom drawer of my desk.

I cleared a spot so I could see the date on my desk calendar blotter where I listed the few weekend deliveries that popped up from time to time. No one would ever accuse me of the kind of organization that used a spreadsheet, but it worked for me.

"Ha!" I said triumphantly. "Just Mrs. Baxtrom's bouquet from Mr. Baxtrom. I think I overheard her say she was going to fly down to someplace warm—probably the Bahamas or someplace like that—for the weekend. You can just leave it with her house help. It'll be an easy day."

I walked over to the cooler and unlocked it. Francis came up behind me with a steaming cup of coffee in his hands. Not having heard him, I nearly jumped out of my skin.

"Oh, so sorry, Patty."

"Heh, heh. I must be needing some more sleep myself," I said.

I pulled out a few of the coral roses Francis seemed partial to and looked for a couple of carnations and the oldest Baby's Breath stems to put with them. After all, if she didn't fly out of town and was around, I doubted she even looked at the weekly bouquet by now. She probably wished she could dispense with it and move on with her life.

"I love these coral ones, Patty," Francis remarked.

"I know."

"Once I get dis delivered, I come back and sing you a lullaby," Francis laughed.

I looked up at him as I tore the green paper off its roll and laid the bouquet in it.

"That coffee sure gave you a lift," I noted as I tied the ribbon.

"I poured you some and put it on the counter for you, see?"

I looked to where he was pointing at the cup, it's steam wafting toward us, a mere three inches from the bottom of the paper.

"It's a winner today, Patty. It's strong, like my mamma used to make it."

I had no doubt that Brazilian coffee or whatever they had down there where Francis had grown up was strong enough to peel the bark off a tree.

"Uh, thanks. I'll get it in a minute," I replied, making a mental note to pour half of it down the drain and add water to the rest after he left.

The phone rang just as the door fell shut behind my esteemed delivery driver with the head-pounding hangover. As I was taking an order for a corsage from someone who had missed the memo that, other than at weddings and proms they went out of style by the time the '60's had come to a screeching close (and, for people like my grandma, not a moment too soon) a man walked through the doors and began to browse.

Now I can tell you, having worked at The Flower Cart for awhile, that sometimes women walk into the flower shop to look around; to breathe in the slightly tangy scent of cut flowers and the detritus—I know, big word; I learned it in college and I'm very proud of it. I try to work it into conversation from time to time, but not with Jess. She gets annoyed. Anyway, as I was saying, the detritus of this business that flower shops call potpourri; they might pick up some little trinket for sale that goes with the whole bouquet idea, they might ask to see a book of arrangements or finger some ribbon; but men don't. A man comes in, walks up to the counter and says what he needs something for. Then he takes what you suggest as long as he can afford it and sometimes when he can't.

As soon as I got off the phone, I took a sip of too strong coffee and pretended to be busy, but I watched the fellow out of the corner of my eye. He wasn't looking at flowers or trinkets or ribbon. Instead, he was knocking the non-merchandise part of my shop to kingdom come. As he passed a wall, he would knock on it nonchalantly, as though he was just tapping a beat he had in his head. His eyes scanned the floor and he picked up urns and pressed the bottoms of them. He ran his fingers over the doors of the cooler where I kept the fresh flowers.

I was doing a pretty good job of pretending not to notice him when he walked up to the counter. The way he looked directly at me—like when someone catches you doing something they disapprove of—made me think maybe I wasn't quite as slick as I'd thought. He picked up a greeting card from the carousel on the counter without examining it and stuck his hand in his pocket. He rummaged around; pulling out two paper clips, a tin of mints, and a receipt in the process, laying them on the counter. He finally pulled out a couple of bucks to pay for it. While I rang up his oh so expensive purchase, he impatiently tapped on the counter with his fingers.

I told him to have a good day, and he left before I noticed he'd accidentally left his pocket lint and everything else on the counter. I ran to the door to call him back, but his car must have already pulled into the traffic of the unseasonably warm November morning. I swooped up the junk, but pulled out the paper clips to put in my desk drawer.

I was just about to toss the rest, when I rethought my action. After all, I didn't usually buy breath mints, them being what I choose to think of as an extravagance, and these looked like they were from some fancy place in the city. That man must have had plenty of dates or business meetings because there were only two left in the tin. I popped one in my mouth and was out like a light.

6

The incessant pounding on my door woke me. I sat up and looked around, trying to clear the cobwebs from my brain. I was lying on top of the covers of my hastily-made bed. Okay, so maybe I'm not the best housekeeper in the world, but I always make my bed, just not to the degree that Martha Stewart would approve. What I couldn't figure out was how I got there.

The pounding was getting a little annoying. If I didn't do something to stop it, the lady down the hall would probably call the police. She called them once just because Mr. Hammerding's cat was roaming the hallway. That's all I needed: the police coming to my apartment. It was bad enough to see them at The Flower Cart and the Bagel Cafe.

Thinking of the Bagel Cafe gave me a sudden thought, and I looked at my night stand where I recalled placing the paper Jess had given me; the one with the map and numbers. It was gone.

I got up from the bed a little too fast apparently, because I felt a headache gradually coming on like a slow simmer.

I stumbled to the door, not bothering to look through the peephole before I unlocked it. Only one person would make such a racket in the middle of the morning.

Jess burst into the room as soon as she heard the click of the lock. She was out of breath, and her face had taken on an interesting shade of peachy-pink.

"Oh my word, Patty! I've been knocking for like," she looked at her watch, "six and a half minutes and before that called and called. What have you been doing?"

"I, I don't . . ."

"And why in the world are you still dressed up?"

If I had actually been dressed up in Jess's world, I would have looked much different, but, being the good friend that she was, Jess knew that in my world 'dressed up' was anything other than jeans or sweats.

I scrunched my eyebrows. Jess must be distracted from a soiree with Bobby buff. She knew I worked Saturdays. Before I could ask her about it, she went to the kitchen and started making some coffee.

I suddenly felt sick, and ran to the bathroom to throw up. I came back out and turned off the coffee maker, pouring the coffee down the drain and throwing the grounds into the wastebasket.

Jess frowned.

I, myself, felt a little undone and plopped onto the couch.

"The smell of the coffee—it just made me feel so sick . . ."

I couldn't continue. My headache had passed the point of simmer and was closing in on a slow boil.

"Would you get me some aspirin, Jess?"

I could hear Jess rummaging around in my medicine cabinet. When I heard her knock the cup that held my razor into the sink, I laid back on the couch. This could take awhile.

* *

I opened my eyes for the second time that day. I must've fallen asleep again. The low light from a corner lamp outlined the form of the person sitting in the chair opposite the couch.

The form leaned forward.

"Patty?" she said in a voice I missed.

I sat up and slapped my feet to the floor like a beaver tail.

"Carly?!" I nearly shouted, then bringing my hand to my temple, said more softly, "Is it you? Really?"

"Quiet. No one knows I'm here."

"But . . ."

"Just listen, okay?" She talked fast, stumbling over her words.

I nodded, then stopped and leaned back on the couch. My headache was mostly gone, but the threat of it still lingered.

"Do you remember when I visited you at the flower shop?"

I closed my eyes.

"Remember? Patty? It was about a week before my parents were killed and a couple or so months before Alden called me for a date."

Wait a minute. Was she talking about over a year and a half ago? I opened my eyes.

"I saw something. I mean, I guess I saw a lot of things all the times I visited, but I didn't know it at the time, and," Carly's eyes were moist and they focused on the wall, listening. She looked at her watch.

"But the last time, I saw a new thing."

She was searching for words that seemed to escape her.

"And . . . and I don't know who to trust other than you. The police, I don't know, there's one I've seen, I don't know . . ." Her voice drifted off.

Then we heard footsteps in the hall one floor below.

"Oh crap. I've got to get out of here. Stay safe, okay?"

She got up and hugged me.

"But, Carly, what? What's going on?"

"I wanted to tell you, but I can't stay right now. I've been here too long. You're one deep sleeper, you know that? I'll try to get back in touch," she said over her shoulder. Love and hopelessness blended together in her voice.

She stopped and laid something on top of the TV.

"I found this. I don't know. Maybe it can help."

Just then someone started slamming his fist into the walls and doors below with the force of a special ops team. Carly's eyes darted around, then, as they landed on me, she ran out the door and flew down the stairs. I heard more yelling and someone being thrown into the wall. It grew quiet before I reached the hallway door.

I shut the door with a shaky hand and leaned against it. Either I was hallucinating or Carly had just visited me—I looked out the window, squinting—in the middle of the night.

I staggered back to my bed and immediately passed out.

7

I overslept and rushed to work. That never happens and I felt rather discombobulated, to say the least. When I got to The Flower Cart, the door was open wide, and Francis was in the back already making coffee which, for some reason, made me feel temporarily nauseated. I ignored it, though, when I spied Mrs. Baxtrom, who was tapping her fingers on the counter like she had to be someplace else and I was holding her back. The minute I stepped over the threshold, she turned and looked at me as though I'd done something wrong.

What was wrong, as far as I was concerned, was that there were two people in my flower shop before I opened it, and I was the only one with a key.

I blew past ye olde Madame, holding up an index finger to let her know I saw her, and, hurrying to throw my purse into my desk drawer, was met by Francis coming out of the back room. He had apparently forgotten who owned this place. Even though he'd been the delivery driver since before I got my high school part-time job with Trudy Tilden, that did not give ol' Francerino the right to jimmy open the lock on the front door of my—and I can't be more firm about this particular fact—*my* store. I was the one, after all, who paid the mortgage on the loan for the dream I hadn't had. Why everything seemed blurry, I couldn't explain just now, but work was work, and this was *mine.*

Before I could express my extreme displeasure, he grabbed my arm, frowning, and asked, "What's wrong, Patty? Why did you leave the store after you opened it?"

I shrugged out of his grasp and shook my head, frowning back at him.

"I'm just opening it now, Francis; or I would be if you hadn't broken in ahead of me."

Francis looked at the clock in the back room just as Mrs. Baxtrom called from the front of the store. Francis and I looked at each other. Mrs. Baxtrom raising her voice was no small matter when it came to the business end of The Flower Cart, her dead husband's flowers being a dependable part of each week's receipts 'n all.

By the time we'd both gone out to take Mrs. Baxtrom's order and I had given her a red rose and baby's breath free of charge for her wait, I'd had time to cool off a little.

"What did you mean when you said I opened the store?" I asked, a little testiness still in my voice.

"I got here at the usual time, Patty. The door was unlocked and I walked in, but you weren't here."

I glared at him.

"I thought you had to go back—I don't know—to your apartment or to the gas station maybe to buy lunch for today."

Likely story, though as the thought pinged in my brain, I knew in my heart of hearts that Francis wasn't the kind to break into anything.

I began straightening the counter. The card carousel was slightly to the left of its usual spot and I automatically nudged it over. Then I remembered the man who had bought a card on Saturday, and slowly began to recall what I had done after that.

I felt Francis staring at me before I saw him, but I already knew what he was staring at, because I could feel the color draining from my face. He was beside me in the nick of time and caught me, preventing what would have no doubt been a clumsy crash resulting in floral paper, scissors, rubber bands, paper clips, and pens on the floor with me unconscious in the middle of them. I leaned on him as we made our way back to my office where I fell into my desk chair.

"Francis, can you dump the coffee for now?" I asked as I tried to think of something other than the smell of dark coffee beans.

"But Patty, dis is fresh. I just made. . ."

"Just do it!"

I heard the newly made, fresh coffee pouring down the drain and the sound of rinse water swishing around in the pot.

I rested both elbows on my desk, put my head in my hands, and closed my eyes, thinking again of Saturday morning.

I could feel Francis standing there, silent and uncertain.

Looking up at him, I shook my head.

"I'll be fine. Why don't you take the rest of the day off. "

"But Patty, what about the deliveries? What about..."

"Okay! Take the deliveries and go. Just go."

He stood there for a minute more, then I heard him grab what I hoped were decent bouquets and leave, the bell on the door tinkling as he walked out.

I got up and, steadying myself, walked around the store, trying to sort things out and remember. I wandered past the refrigerated flower case, ran my fingers over the partially rusted bird cages that I had labeled with the word *rustic* as I passed them, and stood looking out the front doors for awhile. Turning toward the other end of the store, I spied an empty paper coffee cup that someone had dropped on the floor. That cup had been there, having been kicked into a corner probably two weeks before, maybe longer. Bending over to pick it up, I started thinking about Melissa. I'd hired her soon after she'd turned sixteen. How old was she now? My guess was she had one more year of high school before she was out of town in a flash, just like every other eighteen year old was or hoped to be since this town was incorporated. She wasn't the most thorough sweeper, but as long as there were no mice, I was content. Tossing the cup in the wastebasket, I went back to my desk.

Glancing at the clock, I picked up a pen and started scribbling nonsense. 10:15. Wait—how was it already 10:15? I shook my head. Maybe the little spat with Francis had taken longer than it had seemed. Was the clock off an hour? Okay. 9:00 arrived at the Flower Cart. Door unlocked. Francis and Mrs. Baxtrom inside. 8:45 locked my apartment door and left for work. 8:00 got up, passed on coffee and sipped cherry cola while getting dressed for work. 7:59 woke up without the alarm.

I put down my pen. That's funny. As a habit I always set the alarm before I went to bed. I did it without thinking. I was always prompt. Prompt Patty. When I was growing up, my parents—make that my mother, especially—hadn't tolerated lateness. Or maybe I should say they had, but not happily. Until I was around fourteen, I had a habit of running late. Maybe three minutes, maybe thirty. I didn't really think of it as a problem. See, the thing was that I always found just one more thing to do, one more thing that needed attention before I got to the door. Though my mom was always harping about it, she finally let me have it: not by yelling, which she'd already done plenty of in my opinion, but in the form of nothing: nothing being silence. She hadn't called me to hurry up, hadn't told me how many minutes there were until we needed to be somewhere, and hadn't honked the car horn. She hadn't even shaken her head, not that I was there to notice. One day, she just didn't wait for me. I remember it well. I'd run downstairs, excuses spilling from my lips, and all was quiet. And when she returned from the Homecoming game of my freshman year in high school, I was cured. I hadn't been even a minute late since that day.

I looked again at the clock, and realized it wasn't the clock that was off an hour. It was me! I jumped at my involuntary squeak when sudden memories flooded my mind. Carly had visited me in the middle of the night.

Impossible.

I closed my eyes and tried to see what I thought I remembered. She had on dark jeans, maybe tennis shoes, but I wasn't sure about that. I was certain of her shirt, because it wasn't a style she'd worn in high school, and she actually looked pretty gorgeous in it. She had been wearing a dark turtle neck, but not the kind that fits the neck closely. It was the kind that kind of drapes a little. Not a cowl neck, but more of a—I couldn't think of the word; then I thought if I could think of what she wore in such detail, it couldn't have been a dream, could it have?

I sank further down in my chair. Carly. If Carly came to my apartment and it wasn't a dream, and I was pretty sure it wasn't, then that meant she got away. She needed to get away, right? Right? I mean, she couldn't be in on the crime from August 8th. I swallowed.

I brushed away a tear on my cheek as I recalled something else. Someone had thrown her into the wall. I knew it as surely as if I'd seen it. I felt a little sick.

I thought over the parts of the conversation I could remember. She said she had to leave. 'Get out of here'. Wasn't that what she said? Maybe she'd temporarily escaped the person who was sending me those notes every month. But she had the slip of paper that went missing from my night stand. So whoever took it in the first place had been within range of my high school friend. The night at the Bagel Cafe and the present collided in my brain.

I got up and stretched. I walked to the door and looked outside. It was starting to rain; the kind of rain that, like a strict teacher, announces it's time for a test. It begins softly enough, kind of lulling you into the idea that it's a nice time for a nap and when you wake up the sun will be out again. After that, though, it quickly becomes all business and, along with the wind, drives any thought of balmy days straight out of the realm of possibility. And I knew in my heart that for the past year and a few odd months I'd been just pretending to have balmy days. There would be no more balmy days until I got to the bottom of what happened at the Bagel Cafe on August 8th. Until then the kind of rain that turns to sleet would pour down on my little world, and its accompanying strong winds would blow through The Flower Cart.

8

"Hello. Yes, I'm looking for a Trudy Tilden."

"T-i-l-d-e-n," I spelled to the very helpful person on the other end of the phone.

Except this was the fourth very helpful person I was speaking to, and, being the patient person no one has ever known me to be, I was by now drumming my fingers on my desktop like flying hooves at the Kentucky Derby.

"No, as I told the last three people I spoke with, I don't know what her address is. Her former address is . . . yes, exactly."

"What? Oh. Yes. The Flower Cart was the name of her business, but she sold that."

"To me."

"Okay. Again. Patricia Calico."

"C-a-l-i-c-o."

I looked up from the phone as Francis motioned to me with his coffee cup. I had overcome my temporary aversion to the bean after a couple of days, an accomplishment for which my delivery driver appeared to be extremely grateful. He held up the day's route, I grabbed it and signed it, and he went to get himself another cup before starting on the afternoon deliveries. There were only three. Some birthday bash the next town over—a fortunate order, since it required four large arrangements at over a hundred bucks a pop; two separate orders for the same funeral at the Disciples of Christ Church on the other side of town, though I wondered who else would a church be a disciple of anyway, but I let that thought pass on by; and Mrs. Baxtrom's bouquet.

"Um, I don't think so."

"Okay. Well, thanks anyway. And,"

I waved away the cup that Francis was setting down on my desk. I mean, I was tolerating the smell of coffee, but hadn't worked my way back to drinking it yet. What did he think I was: Ironman?

"If you find out later, would you call this number and let me know?"

"Thanks."

I hung up the phone a little more forcefully than I'd intended, and Francis chuckled and shook his head on the way out of my office.

The bell tinkled. A lady and her little boy walked in, then another woman in a pencil skirt, sweater, and boots;

and before I knew it, the afternoon had melted into the early twilight of a November day.

Francis returned with a check from one of the deliveries, and I sent him off to the world of colorful English and spicy food that he lived in. In the quiet, I once again I sat at my desk, staring into space.

Why didn't the forwarding address Trudy Tilden had left me exist—according to the postal service at least? And, for that matter, why had she sold me this business in the first place? I'd always thought she would work until her arthritis got the best of her hands. She couldn't have saved up much over the years, to my way of thinking. What was she living on, anyway? At the time, I hadn't given it much thought, being overwhelmed with the thought of running a business, much less buying one and all. But now that I was thinking of Trudy Tilden, I was curious. I remembered the exact day and time she'd decided to sell. She'd been straightening up at the end of the day, doing the little odd jobs here and there that constitute closing up. She ran a cloth over some shelves, locked the flower cooler, carefully stacked a few pieces of mail and put them in the desk drawer, and turned and offered me the business. Just like that. If she had been considering retirement before then, she hadn't mentioned it.

I pulled the top middle draw of my desk all the way out and set it on the desk. I pulled out every note, every slip of paper, every pen, everything. I was beginning to think that if I had only seen the mail that she'd so carefully stacked when she offered me this place, maybe I'd have an idea about what made her sell. And if I had an idea about what made her sell this place to me, maybe I'd have another piece of information; the piece of information that Carly had tried to tell me about the night she came to see me; about seeing something a week or so before her parents had been killed and several months before Alden had called her for their date.

Although there was sawdust along the grooves on the sides of the desk drawer, there didn't seem to be anything else.

"Hey Pattycake!"

I started at Jess's entrance. Usually I knew the minute she'd pulled into the parking lot, what with her tendency to brake ever so slightly after it was necessary, leading to what I identified as dents on the dumpster and what Jess referred to as my overreaction. I must've been in deeper thought than I thought.

"Reverting back to second grade nicknames, are we?"

"Ha. Better than Jess the Mess."

I silently begged to differ as she flitted to the mini fridge and pulled out half a muffin I'd saved from breakfast.

"I'm just glad to see you back to work. Wow. That must've been some bug. They say the flu has been going around though...."

"It wasn't the flu."

Jess paused mid-chew.

"Well, it sure wasn't an attack of health or—hey! Glad it wasn't the flu then or I'd be regretting this little snack. Yours?" she asked, holding up the empty muffin wrapper.

I grabbed it from her and tossed it in the wastebasket next to my desk.

"Your mooching habits are going to get you in trouble one of these days, Jessica."

"You, my frienderino, should be glad I stopped by here and got you home."

"I'm not home, so."

"Not today, silly. Saturday."

"*You* got me home?"

"Yea. I stopped here to chat and you were wigged out on the floor behind the counter. I grabbed your purse—you shouldn't throw it behind the counter like that, by the way."

"I don't. I always put my purse in the bottom drawer of my desk."

"That's not where it was Saturday. Anyway, I propped you up, got you into my car and brought you back to your apartment. You're kind of heavy to help, you know that? I was lucky to kick The Flower Cart door shut on our way out. You were mumbling, so I thought you knew what was going on. You were pretty sick, though."

"After I visited you the next day and you were still grogged out, I took the car keys from your purse, *walked* over here and drove your car back to your apartment."

Jess tapped both index fingers on her chest.

"I know. Best friend ever. You're welcome."

I ran my hand over my forehead.

"What? No worries. I put your keys back in your purse, Miss Snoozy."

"I think someone slipped me something."

"What?"

"I think I fell unconscious because of something I ate. Or drank."

Jess rolled her eyes.

"I think someone slipped something..."

"Right," Jess snorted, "Where? At the Subway?"

I stared at her, unsmiling.

"Oh c'mon Patty. You're getting paranoid even for you."

"This isn't funny, Jess," I persisted.

Jess pulled a chair over and sat in front of me.

"Look. Even if I believed you, which I don't, what do you want to do, huh? We sorted through possibilities the first night you showed me Carly's picture in your apartment, we racked our brains at the Bagel Cafe, we. . . we. . . well, I can't think of what else, but I don't know what else we can do. If the police department can't figure it out after a year..." Jess's voice trailed off for a minute as some rogue thought—probably of Kent in a tight t-shirt—distracted her.

"I don't know what we can do," she repeated.

I jumped out of my chair and started cleaning the office.

"I do. Let's take a vacation. You and me. Go someplace warm?"

Jess screwed her lips in thought.

"But..."

"Let's get out of here for awhile. Clear the cobwebs."

"And that's supposed to help us figure out the trouble at the Bagel Cafe?"

"Trouble?"

Either Jess was becoming a master of understatement—highly doubtful—or her vocabulary, like Newton's third law of motion, was decreasing with the equal and opposite increase of her stress level.

Jess ignored me.

"That's supposed to help us figure out the mystery of the monthly letters and what laid you flat this past weekend? Which, by the way, I tried to help you, but you were so spacey and sleepy, it was next to impossible. You probably don't even remember me straightening up the place, do you?"

I shook my head.

"But I do recall you knocking my razor cup into the bathroom sink," I said raising my eyebrows to indicate my disapproval. I had to stop, though, because I was afraid thinking about it would bring back the headache from hell and I'd rather it stayed there.

Jess waved me off.

"Or my tucking you into a blanket on the couch after you'd passed out like a drunken sailor?"

"Really," I replied. She said that just to push me into a debate on the perils of alcohol and I wasn't biting. Besides, she agreed with me anyway; she just didn't admit it because doing so would compromise her college babe rep.

"Or my leaving your door unlocked when I left the second time so that if you were still sick the next time I came, my knocking on your door wouldn't bother that lady who called the police on Mr. Hammerding's cat?"

"Huh."

I began thinking of how Carly had been sitting in my living room when I woke up.

"Please don't blame me for taking a day trip with Bobby. I had no idea you were still so sick until I came over on Sunday. Besides, there wasn't much I could have done for you anyway, you being asleep and all."

"Slow down. When did you go out of town with Bobby buff?"

"Oh, he called on Saturday morning," Jess began, crossing her legs and bouncing her foot up and down. "He wanted to check out an antique mall in the middle of nowhere. It was on county 14. Or was it 40? Oh who knows. It had a 4 in it. You're lucky I stopped by the Flower Cart before I left. It did set me back a little, but I still had time to pick up a fruit plate from Lundborg's Grocery Mart."

I half-listened as I tried to piece the weekend together.

". . . then after the antique mall, which was really just a junk-filled barn—though I must admit there was a cute little floral wreath thingy—we had a fall picnic—are you listening?"

I nodded.

" . . . out in the middle of nowhere if you can believe such a thing. It was even comparably warm, but he wrapped us both in a blanket and fed me grapes. Grapes! I know. It was so romantic. And he'd baked vanilla chip scones. Okay. I'm sure they were from a box mix, but still. Are you listening, Patty?"

I looked at Jess and blinked.

"How long were you gone on your—your outing?"

"Oh . . . I don't know. I'd say we were out of town most of the morning. That is, after we'd gotten a little bit of a late start due to me taking you back to your apartment. Then we went to a matinee and finally had supper at a little out of the way place. I couldn't tell you where it was. It was the best date we've ever had. Ever! We were sympatico, you know? That means . . ."

"I know what it means."

Jess sighed with a coo.

"Bobby and Jess—together forever. Patty, why is that pained look on your face?"

"Jess, if one small trip with Bobby was so great, wouldn't a bigger trip with me be even better?"

"Sure! How about spring break on a Florida beach?" Jess laughed.

"How about now?"

Jess got up and looked out the window. "Now? Why?"

"I'll explain on the way there. Warm. Someplace warm," I reminded her.

Jess was beginning to cave, I could tell. It didn't take much for Jess to cave anyway, and the thought of going to a warmer location was doing most of my convincing for me.

"You must have some time coming from that job of yours and it shouldn't take much for you to catch up on any college work you miss. I can close up shop for a week with hardly a squawk, except from Mrs. Baxtrom, and, who knows, she might even appreciate a break from her dead husband's flirtations."

"When were you thinking of going?" Jess asked tentatively.

"The sooner the better."

And that was how we ended up in the first car chase of our lives.

9

"How long has that car been following us?" Jess asked, checking the lock on her door for the fourth time.

I studied the image in my rearview mirror. A black Buick Legacy that I was guessing had all the bells and whistles, though who was I to say for certain, had shown up just as we'd pulled out of town. And though we'd stopped twice, once for gas and snacks for Jess and once for two Burger Kwik mocha lattes, it always reappeared once we were on our way again. First of all, Burger Kwik, right? I mean, I know it's pretty common for most people, but one of the idiosyncrasies of small town living was not necessarily having what was common for most people. So a Burger Kwik latte was right up there with a visit to the White House for us, and I wasn't altogether willing to acknowledge which one we preferred.

"He showed up just as we pulled onto the highway," I said, pressing slightly harder on the accelerator.

"Maybe it's just a coincidence, right?" Jess suggested hopefully, "Like maybe we're just two travelers on the same highway and he happens to be driving behind us."

"And maybe it's just a coincidence that I get a letter every month from somebody talking about The Bagel Cafe thing."

"Well you don't have to get all huffy on me."

Minutes passed as Jess thought it through and her knee started to bounce with increasing rapidity.

"Maybe it's something else. Maybe our tire's low and he wants to get our attention. I heard that in cold weather tires need more air because cold molecules are slower than hot molecules and don't take up as much space."

I tried to think of where in the world Jess had heard that since she knew next to nothing about cars. Maybe fear was actually juicing her brain.

"Or there could be some other reason for him to follow us."

"Yea, Jess, like maybe he wasn't happy with our last order at the Burger Kwik," I replied sarcastically.

As we rode in silence, I looked at the slate-colored sky and wondered if it would eventually provide us with enough snow and wind to hide us, but the day's weather remained achingly dull and boring.

"Do you really think whoever is in the car back there could have something to do with the trouble at the Bagel Cafe?"

"Again with 'trouble'? Really, Jess?"

"Well then, huffy person, what would you call it?"

"Murder?"

"No proof," Jess shot back.

"Mayhem?"

"And we really ever use that word," Jess rolled her eyes.

She had a point there, so I shrugged.

"What if it has something to do with Carly?" I asked tentatively.

"What if whoever is in that car back there was at the cafe that night?" Jess countered, her eyes growing big.

"What if he wants to kill us?!" we both shouted together.

A train whistle sounded in the distance, startling Jess, and she spilled what was left of her latte. Oh, it wasn't an emergency or anything, just a little stain that would meld into the fabric of her already beat up jeans. As she was rummaging in the glove compartment for a wet wipe, I kicked it up a notch. There wasn't much else Jess could spill at that point, and I really didn't want this guy on our tail when it got dark outside. I should've warned her, though, because the glove compartment door somehow slammed shut on a thin little piece of her finger.

Jess's howls rivaled a wolf pack. "This isn't just an inconvenient situation anymore, Patty! Look for a hospital sign! I have to go to the emergency room!" Jess sucked on her finger and dabbed the spot on her jeans with a wet wipe with the other hand.

"I mean it, Patty! Look! I'm bleeding!" She held her finger in front of my face before sticking it back in her mouth. "ER stat! Stat!"

"What makes you think we should put ourselves in a small enclosed space? The maniac following us would just follow us in and we'd be trapped!"

"What if I was bleeding out of my ears?! Would you find a hospital then?!"

"No, I would not, because I'll take possible death over certain death any day!"

I focused on the road. It really does take quite a bit of concentration to drive 90 mph. I tried to keep the needle hovering around there, not wanting to tip the three digit mark, but as the miles passed and the Legacy stayed right on our tail, I was running out of ideas other than moving into warp speed. I'd just begun to ask Jess if she preferred to be called O'Hura or Scottie when a small town appeared in the distance, and its appearance gave me an idea. I'd need to slow down—at least in my world I would slow down. After all who speeds through a small town at break neck speeds unless they want to be stopped by a cop with nothing better to do than sit at a speed trap? There are many things a small town isn't able to provide for its residents, but on the other hand, small town citizens know a few unwritten rules that visitors might not know and speeding ticket revenue is one of them. But the thought of hoping the car behind us would get caught in a speed trap while I nonchalantly drove thirty mph for three blocks gave me another idea. I tapped the break, then breaked hard enough to spin the car in the opposite direction. We hurtled down the highway going the wrong way and passed the black Legacy, with Jess screaming and peering over the seat out the back window. I was too busy wondering if the pack of cars a few miles ahead of us would arrive sooner than I guessed. Those math problems they have you do in school—the ones asking about how fast car A will reach car B if A is traveling X miles per hour and B is traveling N miles per hour—suddenly rushed from the recesses of my memory like the bully they always were; except for now, they were a matter of life and death. Who would think a math assignment could ever in a million years have anything to do with the real world, not that our current predicament felt anything remotely like the real world.

Jess started screaming, "He turned around! He's following us! He's catching up! Patty!!"

Jess started blubbering and the rest of her words were one big multi-syllable occasionally interrupted by shrieks.

I stole a glance in the rearview mirror, and, sure enough, whoever it was that was following us had changed direction and was gaining ground behind us. I swerved left onto a gravel road over which a railroad track passed. I looked right and saw the train that had not long ago been party to the stain on Jess's jeans. And I asked myself if it was better to be hit by a train or caught by someone who at this point in my imagination had reached mythical proportions of law-breaking unknown to man. I gunned the car over the tracks, heard the whistle pierce the air as the train missed us by fewer inches than I would ever admit, and caught sight of the Legacy idling on the other side.

I raced down the gravel road with no idea where we were headed. The sun sets in the west. I knew that much, because I'd learned it from the occasional Western I watched when there was nothing better on. Anyway, at this point, I didn't know where the sun was, much less which direction the road was taking us. The road, and I had no idea if it had a name or a number or a letter as an identifier, had run straight for a short time, then turned and turned again until I'd lost track of the tracks completely. It wasn't like I had the leisure to take my eyes off the road, which was plenty narrow. I would have asked Jess, but as soon as we'd beaten the train, she'd started rummaging through the car looking for something—anything—to eat. I thought I should wait at least until she was finished running her finger around the edges of both of our mocha cups to get the last of the chocolaty flavor.

I decided the best I could do would be to turn at every intersection we crossed.

Finally, Jess calmed down enough to yell, "What are you doing, Patty, figure eights?! If you don't stop, I'm gonna be sick."

"Well I'm not feeling tip top, myself!" I yelled back.

I started feeling better, though, after I slowed down enough to look in the rearview mirror and saw something that was better than an antacid.

"Nothing," I started muttering to myself.

"What?!" asked Jess, still in shouting mode.

"Nothing. Look, Jessica, nothing's there. No one's following us"

Jess careened her neck and started fist pumping the air until she accidentally hit my head and had to apologize.

After that, we decided it would be better not to stop for any longer than it took to buy gas or food. We took turns driving and sleeping, and by the time we got to Florida, we'd had so many Burger Kwik mochas, we'd begun to guess which ingredients made them so appealing. Oh yes. We were living high.

When we crossed the Florida line, I bought a state map at a gas station, and we determined the route we needed to get to Sarasota, the name of the city listed on the forwarding address Trudy Tilden had left for me. When we arrived there, we decided it would just be a matter of tracking down my old boss and asking her some long overdue questions. What were we thinking?

10

"How could you fall asleep at a STOPLIGHT?!"

"Did you want to drive? Because you can drive, you know, even though I didn't say anything when you veered onto the shoulder that last time."

"I was trying to miss an armadillo."

"I saw it. It wasn't worth missing."

"Never-mind. We don't have that much further to go anyway. Oh look! A Burger Kwik!"

I was miffed, but also hungry, so what could I do?

We stopped for a breakfast that didn't help our spirits as much as one might imagine. I'm sure it had nothing to do with our non-stop cross-country travel. I was again at the wheel which meant we were at the mercy of Jess and the map. No. No we didn't have GPS. Go ahead and gloat at our small town ways, but until this trip we'd never used it. We tried to use the one on Jess's phone, but had finally grown so irritated with the lady giving us bad directions that we'd shut it off.

We had arrived in town late enough for the motel clerks to think they could take advantage of us by raising their prices. What could we say? We'd driven a straight shot from north to south and we looked it; so we did what any cheap person of a certain age would do and found an out of the way place to park the car and sleep as comfortably as the transients we appeared to be could. No one had stopped and shined a blinding flashlight in our faces and we'd actually gotten a decent night's rest. We even changed our clothes, a blessing to the one with fresh clothes, the one riding with her, and anyone else who might happen to come within three feet of us.

We'd lucked out by stopping at a grocery store and looking at the bulletin board by the front doors while we munched on some fig cookies we'd bought there. There was a small ad for a flower sale along with an address, and for some reason the way the plants were combined in the ad—three here, two there, and so on—reminded me of Trudy Tilden. I know. It was a shot in the dark and my crazy imagination both. Still. The paper was old enough to be yellowed and brittle and was torn on the corner, but what did we have to lose?

I was beginning to feel renewed hope in finding my old boss now that we were in the land of swamps and alligators. Jess and I had discussed this while we did the whole clothes change thing. First of all, was it really alligators? Or was it crocodiles? Secondly, we each had heard plenty about little dogs getting caught up in one bite and taken to their final resting place by some hungry gator. Or croc. Oh yea, we could abbreviate with the best of Floridians. As Jess pointed out and I agreed, being down in the ol' southerino of the good ol' U. S. of A. was beginning to make us feel like natives of all things Everglade. We ignored the fact that our only exposure to such a thing was in the form of the room freshener they used in the bathroom at the movie theater. Anyway, we weren't about to get suckered into the gator/ croc problem, which was why we were both wearing sturdy running shoes and not the flip flops we would have preferred. My feet were already hot and sweaty.

"It's off of Fruitville Road, I said."

Jess paused.

"Or University Parkway. Um, or Bee something or other."

"Believe? Before?"

"How about be quiet!" Jess huffed.

"Thank you, Jessica. Thank you for your fine map reading skills," I mumbled irritably.

* *

"Ha. There it is!" Jess cried jubilantly as I whizzed past the address we were searching for.

I turned around in the next parking lot, and headed back the way we came. Actually I didn't pull in and out quite so quickly, because it was, amazingly enough, a Burger Kwik and, upon seeing the sign, Jess decided to get an iced coffee first.

Even if we didn't find Trudy Tilden, this was turning out to be a great vacation. We were getting our fill of all kinds of fast food. I know, I know. Most of the population is blasé—look at me branching out from pretend Spanish to French—about that sort of thing, but to that I reply, *small town*.

"Why are we looking for your old boss again?"

Jess was already at the point of slurping her iced coffee from the bottom of the cup.

I pulled in front of the address we'd been looking for and parked.

"Because I want to find out why she sold me The Flower Cart and why she moved so far away so fast. I mean, at first, though it seemed to come out of the blue, I didn't think much about it. But with that man coming into my shop last Saturday and then Carly visiting me in the middle of the night and telling me she saw something, I'm beginning to think something's off with more than just The Bagel Cafe."

"Whoa!" Jess immediately locked her car door and started rummaging through the duffle bag by her feet. She pulled out a small hand gun and held it up to examine it.

"What in the world?! Are you trying to kill us? Put that away, for pete's sake!"

Jess raised her eyebrows at me, an indication she thought I was crazier than she was.

"First off," she said, resting her gun in her lap as though it were a newborn, "the gun isn't loaded. I've taken gun safety classes because I am a responsible gun owner. One of the rules is, and I quote, 'ALWAYS keep the gun unloaded until ready to use'."

She started rummaging around for her box of ammunition, laid it on the top of the things in her bag, and huffed at me. I knew what the huff meant. It meant she thought I was a little lamb being led to the slaughter by the anti-gun radicals. I didn't feel like arguing with her just then. After all, I wasn't feeling exactly safe and secure after the car chase from hell.

"Secondly, I know how to use it. I just think of bras."

"Oh now you're just making things up."

Jess tilted her head at me accusingly. "Am not. You're supposed to breathe, relax, aim, squeeze. Bras."

I put my hands over my ears, but Jess reached over and pulled them down again as her words came faster.

"Thirdly, you didn't tell me anything about a man in your shop. And finally," she continued, holding up her hand to stop my interruption before it started, "CARLY?!"

I cleared my throat.

"I didn't want you going spastic."

Jess tilted her head and her eyes drilled into mine with a level of frustration that was ready to blow up any minute.

"Okay, okay. I told you I thought I was drugged, but not at a local restaurant like you so kindly and sarcastically suggested."

I let out a long breath, leaned my head back on the headrest, closed my eyes, became as still as a school building in July, and watched it all over again in 3-D.

"A man came into The Flower Cart that Saturday and was looking around . . ."

"Why would a man look around a flower shop?"

"That's what I thought. And he was knocking on the walls and stuff. Pressing his fingers on things. Running his hands on the edges of things. Then he saw me looking at him and he bought a card."

Jess's voice was doubtful.

"Why would he buy a card because you were looking at him?"

"And when he paid for it, he pulled everything out of his pocket and there was lint and stuff, right?"

"Okay."

"And a couple paperclips and whatever."

"Aw," Jess crooned, knowing what paperclips made me think of.

"Not now, Jess. And a tiny tin of mints. But he forgot to put them back in his pocket before he left. And I scavenged what I could including . . ."

"The paperclips?"

"Yes. And the box of mints. They looked like they were from some fancy place."

"Which fancy place?"

"I don't remember. But I put one in my mouth because why not."

"Why not?" I could hear Jess's knee pounding up and down like a jackhammer, and her gun falling to the floor.

"And that's all I remember."

"What do you mean that's all you remember?"

"Because, Jess, everything's a blank after that. I think it was a drug that knocked me out."

I could hear Jess's open-mouth breathing.

"That's when I found you?"

"I don't know how long after, but yes."

"And brought you back to your apartment?"

"Yes. And left the door unlocked Sunday after you came back to check on me. And Sunday night I woke up and Carly was just sitting there . . ." I peeked over to see how Jess was taking all of it.

She was fanning herself with her iced coffee cup. I closed my eyes again.

". . . trying to say something that I didn't really understand and she left that slip of paper you gave me when we were at the Bagel Cafe trying to remember everything."

As I wrapped up my little soliloquy and opened my eyes, Jess's face had turned a light shade of green.

I know. Soliloquy, right? I love that word. It's like a spoken song. Solo and, and, quy. Okay, so I admit quy doesn't mean 'spoken'. It means 'precious'. I learned that from the Vietnamese guy who sat next to me in freshman English when I still thought I'd get a college degree and he still thought I'd be impressed by his calling me a name in a different language.

"So you weren't sick after all? You really were drugged?! With mints?!"

"If you ever say I've touched a drug, Jess, so help me I will never speak to you again. It doesn't count if it was an accident."

"Of course it doesn't," Jess said, still fanning herself.

The color was beginning to come back to her face, a good sign as far as I was concerned, considering there was nowhere for her to get sick other than the curb or my car.

"Were they minty?"

This is why Jess and I had remained friends all these years. We helped each other remember the important details of life.

"I don't know, Jess," I said quietly. "I passed out, remember?"

"You don't need to start sounding like a Cold War spy. I was only curious."

"I think we'd better knock on the door before someone reports us for stalking," I said, looking at the house from our curbside parking place.

"But do you remember anything about getting back to your apartment after you'd passed out?" Jess whispered as we walked up the steps.

"No memory."

I rang the bell and a woman with bleached hair opened the door. The flash of recognition in her eyes gave her away. When she was the owner of The Flower Cart, Trudy had blended in with every other Midwesterner of a certain age. Maybe she'd gone blonde because she was now living in the land of the snow birds. She looked ten years younger. I might not have recognized her on the street.

She gasped, looked both ways up and down the street and pulled us in, locking the door behind us.

11

Trudy Tilden patted her chest with a fluttering hand and motioned for us to follow her to her kitchen.

"We were in the area and thought we'd stop by to see my former boss."

I chuckled as I said it to make it sound believable and friendly.

"Is that right?"

"Um hm. You must wonder from time to time how everything is going."

Trudy didn't answer.

"Don't you?"

"Oh! Yes. Yes."

"The Flower Cart has a steady business," I said as I looked around the living room we passed through on our way to the kitchen.

Jess hung back, glancing into what appeared to be a small bedroom, but hurried forward when I frantically waved my hand down low for her to keep up.

"Good. Good."

"So do you keep your hands in the flower business down here?"

"Hm?"

"Are you involved in the flower growing, selling, whatever down here?"

"I'm out of the business, but I'd never let gardening go completely, Patty. I like it too much."

"You must miss The Flower Cart then."

We were in her kitchen now, and I kept carrying on the mostly one-way conversation.

"You must've saved more than anyone knew to move so far. I like your house."

"Saved?" Trudy cleared her throat. "Yes. Yes, it's as you said."

"By the way, why did you sell it to me? So quickly an' all?"

Trudy Tilden must not have heard me, though, because she busied herself at the kitchen counter and started whistling a tune without much of a melody.

Once we were sitting in her chrome dinette chairs and sipping on some sweet tea, once she'd pulled down her shades even though twilight was hours away, once she'd squinted her eyes at us as though we were a pair of some kind of rare marmosets, she said, "I can't believe my eyes! What brings you and your friend . . ."

"Jessica," Jess filled in the blank.

". . . Jessica to Sarasota?"

Jess gazed longingly at the oatmeal cookies in a clear jar on the counter.

Trudy Tilden didn't notice. She shook her head as though it was a throw rug and today was cleaning day. "How did you find me, Patty?"

"I didn't know you were hiding."

Trudy tittered for close to five seconds, which may not sound like a long time, but it feels suspicious when you're hearing it.

"Oh no! No. Of course not! Why would I hide? Why in the world would I hide? No, Patty. I meant I didn't know you had my address."

"You gave me an address, Ms. Tilden, but . . ."

"Oh please, Patty. We're both business women now. Call me Trudy."

". . .Trudy, but the Post Office said the address, the one you gave me, doesn't exist."

Trudy put her hand on her chest again.

"Is that so?"

We both sat silently looking at each other, apparently having nothing else to say. Except Jess. She would have said something, but it isn't good manners to ask for something to eat when you're a guest, so instead she just kept looking at the cookie jar.

"We saw an old ad for a plant and flower sale and for some reason it made Patty think of you," Jess finally said, giving up the oatmeal cookie hint and gulping her sweet tea.

"Oh dear," Trudy whispered. She looked up, "Where did you see it?"

Jess, warming to the subject, gave her the name of the grocery and its approximate location.

Trudy frowned and started playing with the hem of her dress.

"I need to talk with you, Trudy, because some things have been happening back home that are causing me some trouble."

Jess smirked at me. Okay, I know had told her 'trouble' didn't even begin to describe what had happened at the Bagel Cafe, but I didn't feel like giving a blow by blow to Trudy who, to be honest, didn't seem that glad to see us.

I gave Jess the sideways look of death and she bit her lip, but not before she added helpfully, "It doesn't have anything to do with mints, though."

Trudy studied us for awhile and then took a long drink of her tea. She seemed to have made a decision, but apparently it didn't have to do with answering my concerns, since the next thing out of her mouth was, "We do have some mint down here, though the chocolate mint I prefer doesn't grow well in this yard."

"As I was saying . . ."

"I," she paused, "I have a suspicion someone grows something from the Cannabaceae family ten or so miles from here.

I've noticed it as I drive past. I suspect they think it blends in with their mint, but it doesn't; at least not to the trained eye. "

Trudy always had muttered Latin that no one understood but herself.

She changed the subject, "Did you know The Flower Cart used to be the space for a vacuum repair shop?"

I shook my head. I suppose I should have cared. Did they include little history lessons like that on a contract? Did it matter? Were there things about the building I should know and didn't? Maybe I should pull out the old contract and read it word for word. Who was I kidding? Of course I wouldn't. Contracts have to be one of the most boring things in the world.

"A vacuum repair shop," I echoed, probably sounding as doubtful as I felt.

"We do, however, have some beautiful flowers down here. Have you noticed the vivid colors? They're lovely!" She thought for a moment, "But I always say not every flower should be sold. Some should just be admired. Cherished even."

Jess nodded her head. She was probably still hoping to get in Trudy Tilden's good graces enough to be offered a cookie.

"Yes, lovely, but about the things back home . . ."

"Oh I do miss the Fall colors back home. Hurricane season here is a bit unsettling depending on the forecast you know, but my arthritis doesn't act up as much in this warm climate."

"That's one thing," Trudy continued as I took a breath to try again, "about the nice weather. The little animals don't suffer so much."

Was that a tear in her eye? No, I was imagining things. I was pretty sure Trudy wasn't one of those who spent time watching sweet little pet videos.

"There's a little neighborhood cat that thinks it belongs to everybody. She comes to my back doorstep every Thursday and if I don't have her can of tuna out, she just howls to beat the band!"

"The trouble!" I nearly yelled as I tried to get my answers. "There was a man in The Flower Cart awhile back . . ."

Trudy Tilden drew a sharp breath.

"Well, dear, you should know by now that men do come in a flower shop . . ."

"But he was checking it out. I mean, he didn't really seem interested in buying anything. He was knocking on the walls, running his fingers up and down the edges of the cooler . . ."

Trudy's face went white and she started making doodle marks on the table with her finger.

"You know, speaking of trouble," Trudy slowly strung out the words as though they would prevent the conversation from going further. "I had some car trouble several weeks ago. How's The Flower Cart truck? Still running well?"

I nodded.

" You wouldn't think there would be vehicle problems down here where we don't have to worry about road salt and the like, but . . ."

"We think he might be—trouble," I said helplessly.

"Or looking for something."

I could hardly believe Trudy had actually given a meaningful reply.

A pained expression flitted across her face as she stared into her lap; then she got up abruptly, wrote something on a two by two card, and slid it into my hand.

"What do you mean, looking for . . ."

"I'm sorry to cut your visit short, but I have a doctor's appointment to get ready for. He might have to prescribe something. Doctors can do that, you know."

"Prescribe something?"

She nodded. "Yes. Prescribe."

She was leading us to the front door. Jess looked back wistfully at her half-full glass of sweet tea and the unoffered oatmeal cookies still in the canister.

"I don't think it's anything—just a little cold. It's so hard to find a decent pair of wool socks down here. Would you mind . . . I'd like to . . . to keep some sense of privacy. So, Patty," she touched my arm, "Don't share my address. Even with Francis or any of the customers or anyone," Trudy laughed lightly. "Please?" she looked me in the eye, and I gave her a half-nod. Then she closed the door behind us.

The lock clicked, and I noticed a small corner of the curtain move. It appeared I wouldn't find out from Trudy Tilden any information including why she sold me her store. At least not today, and we didn't have time to lollygag in Sarasota waiting for her to change her mind. I got in the car and looked down at the small card in my hand. *Bigger than it seems* on one side and *equipment* on the other. I shook my head. Of course I knew this was big. I'd driven to Florida trying to figure it out, hadn't I? And I might not do it to her satisfaction, but I already knew that I should take care of my equipment.

12

"You'd think she would've at least offered us a cookie."

We were following I-75 north and had been driving for twenty minutes. There were some things Jess just didn't let go. She hung on to them until they were threadbare and there was nothing to hang on to anymore. I know, I know, I have those threadbare sweatpants I insist on wearing, but those are things you can actually touch. When I say 'things' in regard to Jess, I mean things she thinks about way beyond the time they should be allotted. In my world, oatmeal cookies should get about ten seconds, eleven if raisins are involved. In Jess's world, well let's just say there's a girl from our sophomore year of high school who has no idea of the danger she's in if she ever comes within spitting proximity of Jess. It isn't likely, though. The girl went off to college in California and has shown no signs of coming back to our little town even for holidays.

"Maybe she was saving them for the neighborhood cat."

Jess frowned.

"The one that howls to beat the band?"

Jess squinted at me.

"If it doesn't get its tuna?" You would've thought she wasn't even there for the conversation. Okay, I admit it. Jess's mind being somewhere other than where everyone else's minds were was clearly within the realm of possibility.

Jess huffed. "That woman was hiding something. Anyone who has oatmeal cookies and doesn't share them shouldn't be trusted."

"Hey, look, Jess, a Burger Kwik." I had to get her mind off cookies before her whole brain became one big oatmeal mush.

"Perfect! I'm starving!"

"Now there's a shocker," I muttered as I took the exit and turned in at the sign marked ENTER.

I was lucky to find a parking spot, even though it was next to a large garbage can. We got our food, decided to take some time to enjoy the ambience of a Florida parking lot and settled down on one of the picnic tables placed just next to it.

"What do you think she means by this?"

I handed Jess the card Trudy Tilden had slipped into my hand.

Jess squinted at it, her lips moving as she read each word. She flipped it over and squinted again.

"Equipment? She did say she still loved gardening," Jess said in between bites of lettuce and spicy ketchup. "I don't get it."

"Neither do I. Did she seem a little skittish to you?"

"Use English, Patty."

"Like she was a little nervous or something?"

"No. She just seemed selfish. You'd think someone with a whole jar of oatmeal cookies could spare one or two. I mean, really, Patty. What was her problemo?"

I friend punched Jess on the arm. Despite her oatmeal cookie grudge, the old Jessica mystique was back.

We watched as two cars pulled out of the lot and another pulled in to the parking space next to mine.

"She didn't even ask about The Flower Cart."

"I know! You would've thought she never owned it! At least she could've asked whether Mrs. Baxtrom was still getting her dead husband's flowers every week."

"Right! Or what about Francis?"

"The ol' Francerino!"

"She could've wondered how he was doing."

The sting I'd first felt at Trudy Tilden's seeming lack of interest in her old business was growing, and I started getting, for lack of a better word, really miffed.

I crumpled up my sandwich wrapper and tossed it toward the garbage can. I missed, of course, and walked over to pick it up. The iron container painted a dark green nearly blended in with a group of trees on the edge of the lot. As I reached for the wrapper, my eyes met a pair of wide, scared, very familiar eyes.

I opened my mouth to yell, but Carly put her finger to her lips and motioned to the door handle of the car she was looking out of.

I nodded, opened the door, and Carly jumped out so fast she nearly knocked me over. I ran to get Jess while Carly opened the rear passenger door of my car and climbed in.

"Jess."

"Why are you whispering?" Jess asked in between final slurps of her soda.

"I'm not whispering. I just think it's time to leave."

"But I was thinking we should get a caramel sundae for the road. Don't you think ice cream would taste good? After all, we didn't get even one cookie."

I jerked my head toward the car. Jess frowned. The thing is, Jess might love the whole idea of a cloak and dagger experience, but there are things about her that really aren't cut out for intrigue.

"Ow!" she yelled as I pulled her up by the elbow.

"Walk, Jess. No. Don't look around. Just walk."

"What has gotten into you, Patty?"

"I'll tell you when we get to the car."

There was no sense in sending Jess into a panic that would be evident to everyone inside the fast food restaurant as well as heard within a two mile radius.

We climbed into the car and I pulled out of the parking lot like a college boy at a frat party.

"Whoa! This isn't the Daytona 500, Patty! You've had too much caffeine. Let me drive."

"I had one cola with my burger. You had one cola, one refill, half a glass of tea, and an iced coffee before that. So, no, I will do the driving for now."

I didn't dare tell her yet who was sitting on the floor behind her less than a foot away because we were still working our way back onto the interstate and I didn't need the distraction of a screaming passenger until I could find some clear road and hit cruise control. Carly's memory of the three of us together, including distinct personality traits that needed no mention, appeared to have remained intact because she stayed crouched and quiet.

We'd settled into a few miles per hour above the speed limit and I was trying to think about how to broach the subject of our missing friend showing up seven states away. I mean how do you even ask that question—especially with my own little stress bomb riding beside me?

Jess was still a little huffy. I didn't say it, but we both knew she was mad about not getting her caramel sundae, probably with nuts, before we left.

I breathed in and out slowly a couple of times and glanced out the window. It seemed impossible that everything looked so normal. But the way things look isn't always the way things really are.

"What got into you back there?"

"Um, I just wanted to get on the road, that's all."

"She was doing me a favor," Carly chimed in as she slid from the floor onto the backseat, shoving some of Jess's things out of the way.

Jess jumped at the sound of her voice, turned backwards in her seat, and began screaming.

"Thanks for waiting until I got out of traffic, Carly."

"No problemo," she laughed as she hugged the still shrieking Jess.

"Jess, you're going to have to calm down so we can get some bearings here!" I yelled.

I had to. Jess had stopped screaming and begun squealing. There was no telling when she would quiet down. In fact, it was entirely possible we would be hearing Jess's entire upper register until we got back home or went deaf, and, having already lost the left side of my own personal surround sound, I wasn't completely comfortable with the possibility I thought would come first.

Jess finally quieted down enough for regular conversation and I asked Carly what we both wanted to know.

"How in the world did you end up in the car parked next to my car? Where have you been? Who were you with? Are you safe? Are *we* safe? What did you see when you visited me at The Flower Cart? Do you know what happened the night of August 8th?

13

Carly looked out the rear window and both windows left and right. Her eyes had a hunted look and she was rocking back and forth. I caught her eye and nodded with as much reassurance as I could fit into it.

We drove in silence for a few minutes until Carly's eyes started looking more like the ones we were used to and her rocking back and forth slowed to a stop. Jess's leg continued to jiggle up and down, but what else could be expected?

"Can I just relax for a minute? Do you know how good it is to see you guys?"

I glanced back at her.

"I mean besides the night I visited you, Patty."

I let out a breath that felt like I had been holding it since that night.

"At least now I have proof I wasn't imagining it."

Carly sighed, "No. No imagination needed."

She rubbed her right eye.

Then she started crying. Little tears at first, then short breaths with the tears, then outright sobbing. Jess climbed into the back seat to cry with her. For the next 30 minutes I drove and Jess held Carly while she sobbed on Jess's shoulder. Finally, with an exhausted sigh, she leaned back on the seat and closed her eyes. Jess had begun stuffing Carly's used Kleenex into a plastic bag we still had from the grocery store. Carly moved it from the seat to the floor.

"I'm sorry. I feel better now, though."

We all breathed a sigh of semi-relief. Sure, she felt better now, but who was kidding who? There were probably more sobbing sessions in our future.

"What I want to know is how was your date with Alden?" Jess asked as she climbed back into the front passenger seat.

Carly and I both looked at Jess like she was out of her mind, which, let's be honest, was altogether possible on more than one occasion, so we had history on our side.

"What? Wait. That's when it all started isn't it?"

When she said it like that, it didn't seem an unreasonable starting point after all.

Carly closed her eyes and a little smile tugged at the corner of her mouth as she filled us in on her getting ready and his picking her up and her tripping and his catching her and, yes, he did touch her back, but no, there was no hand brushing or kissing, what did we think she was—a floozy? Then she sighed with the quietness we barely heard.

"We'd settled in at the theater when . . ."

"Did he get you popcorn?"

Jess was intent on getting all of the information.

"Um, he offered, but I said no."

"No?! Why in the world . . ."

"Jessica!" we both yelled at the same time.

"Jess, thank you for your interest and I promise I'll tell you everything, but I'm still a little shaken up from finding you guys and I just need to say everything and then open it up for questions, 'kay?"

Jess looked a little pouty, but nodded her head. Carly leaned up on the console between us.

"As I was saying, we'd settled into our chairs at the theater and sat through the previews and everything. It seemed like Alden was nervous about something—he kept looking around—and then I thought maybe he was nervous about being on a date with me, right?"

We both tried to nod in agreement, but that would so not be true. Alden was Mr. Perfect and, as much as we loved Carly, she was—not. Our nods kind of got stuck at the half-way point. We were nothing if not honest with each other. Carly didn't seem to notice.

"We sat through maybe thirty or so minutes of the movie, when Alden reached in his pocket and took out a note. And

I thought, 'what?' I mean a note either means a love note or a break up note and it was too early for either of those, right?

Jess and I nodded, and I could tell Jess was biting her tongue like nobody's business, because one of the first things out of Carly's mouth already had her mentally dramatizing either an amazing love story or a jerk move to end all jerk moves. Carly could tell it, too, and took pity on her.

"Okay, Jess. What?"

"What did the note look like? Was it all pretty and perfumy or—no, wait."

She lowered her voice half an octave. "Was it musky? You know, the kind of musky scent the caveman colognes have?"

"I didn't notice. It was just—ordinary, I guess. I didn't notice the color or whether it smelled like anything."

"Please, Carly, can we keep this thing moving? We only have sixteen hundred miles before we're home and I'd like to hear everything before then."

"Okay, crabbypants," Jess said, digging in her duffle bag for something to eat.

After all, a whole sixty minutes had passed since we'd eaten an entire meal.

She passed around a bag of broken dill pickle flavored potato chips as Carly continued.

"Anyway, he had a little flashlight he held on it so I could see it. Wasn't that nice?"

"Oh wow, oh wow, oh wow." Jess was clearly in the moment.

"I opened it up and it said—okay, now this is where it gets crazy, so take some deep breaths."

We both dutifully breathed in and out three times and, after Jess had stopped choking on the chip crumb she'd inhaled, nodded for her to continue.

"So the note said I saw something when I was visiting you, Patty, at The Flower Cart and that it had to do with something about drugs or trafficking or something and that my life was in danger and the FBI wanted to put me in something like a witness retention . . ."

"Witness protection . . ." Jess offered.

We both looked at her.

"What? I read. I watch detective shows."

Okay, her watching detective shows did make sense.

". . . Witness protection thing and was I willing to go with them. I just looked at him like was this a joke or what, you know?"

Boy, did we know.

"And then we just sat there because I didn't know what to do. Or say. And then he touched my arm . . ."

"Oh, he touched your arm!"

Jess couldn't help herself.

". . . and got up and so I got up and followed him out of the theater. We hadn't even gotten to the good part either."

I rolled my eyes. Jess nodded sympathetically.

"When we got outside the theater, there was a guy there that Alden said was his older cousin, Sam."

"Wait wait wait. Did Sam happen to go into the Bagel Cafe at anytime do you know?"

I felt like this was finally one connecting piece of information. Jess was nodding her head up and down like a bobblehead doll.

Carly shrugged. "How would I know? I only saw him outside of the theater. As soon as we stepped out of the building, he took charge. He said he was an agent with the FBI and was I willing to testify about what I'd seen which, I've got to tell you, I still had no idea what he was talking about, and I could come with him to a safe place."

"I don't get it. Why didn't Sam just go to your home instead of having the whole date with Alden thing?" I thought it was a practical question.

Carly and Jess looked at me like I was the most insensitive person in the world other than our old middle school principal.

"Maybe Alden wanted an excuse to ask her out," Jess countered.

Carly shrugged, "I . . . I guess I thought he wanted to ask me out. Now that you mention it, I don't know why Sam just didn't go to my house unless . . ." Her voice drifted off into the land of unspoken possibilities.

"I'm sorry, Carly. Of course he wanted to ask you out."

Who was I to say he didn't have a secret crush on her? Or maybe I was jealous of one of my best friends going out with Mr. Perfect Athletic guy, but I discarded that thought right away. Close proximity was good enough for me, and we all knew it. My big aim as far as romance was concerned reached only as far as the kind of Mr. Right who was slightly rumpled and had an old baseball card collection.

"No. No, Patty. You have a point. In fact, it backs up something that I've wondered about since I've been gone, but . . ."

"Tell us later," Jess encouraged her, patting her knee with one hand and slapping my arm with the other.

Carly let out a loud sigh. "And then we just followed him across the street to the Jeep Alden had driven."

Carly sat back and ate a handful of chips. Who could blame her? This was a lot for us to take in and it must've been a lot for her to unload. Jess had started tapping her foot, and I was beginning to stare into space—not a good thing when you're driving. Carly's face was getting a little hot. We all needed a minute to calm down and we all took it.

"I am so thirsty," Carly croaked. "Do you guys have anything to drink?

"We have a case of water in the trunk," I volunteered.

By this time it would be the temperature of hot cocoa that's been sitting on the table for twenty minutes, but thirsty is thirsty. I pulled into a wayside rest so I could pop the trunk and get the water. Nothing bad ever happens at those places.

14

That's not really true. All three of us had heard all kinds of stories about the terrors of wayside rests. Someone might be in their car resting by the wayside and bam! They're assaulted by some thug who thinks stealing from people is okay as long as he can get away with it. That kind of thinking isn't limited only to Socialists, you know. But thanks to Jess's bag of broken chips making us parched enough to choke, we all were thirsty enough to risk it.

"We need a potty break anyway. Patty, why don't you stay here and watch for the guys that had Carly while we take a moment?"

"I will watch for the guys who had Carly while they come right over and slash us to pieces! For heaven's sake, Jess, I have no idea what they look like."

Jess ignored me while she and Carly bounded out of the car the minute it was in park. I turned a 360 degree circle and, seeing no suspicious-looking persons, unlocked the trunk and pulled out six bottles of water. It was an armful.

I was transferring them to the backseat when Carly said, "I'm back. Go! Go!"

I went, and we were back on the interstate in a matter of six or so minutes. We were all more than a little spooked by this thing we didn't understand, but were in the middle of or, if not in the middle, somewhere along the periphery. I think it's safe to say we were proud of ourselves for such a quick stop. Once Carly had taken some sips of water, her face wasn't so pink anymore, and we all settled back to pick up her story where she'd left off.

"So you got into the Jeep then?" I asked.

I was feeling vindicated about seeing Alden's Jeep and gave Jess an 'I told you so' face.

"We were headed that way," Carly said slowly, "but all of a sudden there was some sort of commotion in The Bagel Cafe, and when Sam and Alden looked over at what was going on, someone grabbed me from behind, stuffed me into a car, and took off. I don't know what happened with Sam and Alden after that."

Jess's eyes were as big as Frisbees.

"Who grabbed you?! What did they do to you?!" Jess's voice was edging to the upper register again. It would be better to bring things down a notch and I gave Carly a sideways glance.

"Look at me, Jess," she reassured her, "I'm here. With you. I'll tell you what happened, but you're going to have to chill a little."

"But Carly, we were in The Bagel Cafe that night," I said.

"Get out."

"We wanted to see how it worked out with you and Alden."

"Aww."

Jess chimed in, "We had you married and everything before things got crazy."

"Oh Jess, I'm so sorry for you for things to have gotten crazy. Are *you* okay?"

"She was in the bathroom the whole time," I said.

Things were getting a little too warm and fuzzy considering we were discussing criminal activity.

"Like I said, I don't know what happened in The Bagel Cafe. I was sitting in the back of a car speeding down the street so fast I was getting thrown back and forth at every turn. The guy driving was the scariest guy I'd ever seen. After a couple of days, I found out his name was—well I don't really know what his name is, I guess. Everyone calls him Gunns. But don't worry," Carly added, looking at me, "it wasn't because of guns guns. It was because of his muscles."

That was so nice of her to remember I was against guns. It just shows you what a nice friend Carly really is.

"The guy sitting in the back seat with me was Mike. I was really sorry to take off on him like that down at the Burger

Kwik, but when I saw you guys—and I hardly could believe I was seeing you, believe me—nothing could've stopped me from taking the chance while it was there."

"You were with Mike, is it? In Florida." I had to repeat it back to her. It didn't make sense she was still with the fellow who pushed her into a car.

Carly froze, and she stared into space before looking at us again.

"With. Mike." Did she need me to spell it out?

"Please believe me. I didn't want to be friends with those guys. As I said, Gunns was scary and a couple of the others were creepy. The only reason they kept their hands off me—well, mostly—and not before they sold me for awhile but let's not talk about that part now—I just want to feel like I'm breathing clean air first—but it was because they thought Mike had a thing for me, which he let them think because I think he really did. They took me to a house—and I'm guessing here—about fifteen, maybe twenty-five minutes outside of town. I don't know for sure, what with getting thrown back and forth in the car. I didn't even see what it looked like that first night because it was so dark. They kept me in an equipment shed by the house."

"Oh no no no," Jess said, but we couldn't really hear her. It was more like she was mouthing the words.

"It had a cot and it was wired, so I could use a space heater and fan they had out there. After I'd been there maybe three months they let me outside sometimes with Mike and even in the house on really cold nights or hot days. It was just kind of a blah house . . ."

"Blah like beige or blah like a rectangle?"

Jess had recovered slightly from Carly's last revelations. Considering the situation, it was surprisingly possible Jess's thing for stupid details now might actually be of some use, even if it did drive us crazy.

"Blah like both, and I *think* it was down that gravel road that you cross on your way out of town. You know the one. The one by the bridge with the sign."

We nodded. We knew exactly which one she was talking about.

"But maybe not. I don't know. Maybe. Maybe not. But then it was like twenty more minutes after that. Or maybe thirty."

We were making all kinds of progress.

"During those first few days I found out he's . . ."

"Who?" we both asked at the same time.

"Mike. He's a year younger than us. He told me he'd seen me in high school before he dropped out. But Gunns is his brother and it was a family thing. He did whatever the rest of them told him to do."

Carly opened another water bottle and drank half of it. She was probably wishing it was something stronger than water. I didn't blame her.

"Then I started thinking about our psych class and how prisoners get that thing where they sympathize with their captors."

"Stockholm Syndrome," I volunteered.

"You always did have a good memory."

Jess nearly choked on her water.

"I think the police might disagree with you on that."

"Puh" I blew my lips at Jess.

"Go on."

"Well I was thinking why can't it work the other way? I mean why does it always have to work only one way, you know?"

"Because they're the ones who decide whether you eat or sleep or get beat up?" I asked. Obviously someone hadn't been listening that closely in class.

"I thought that was for brainwashing."

Carly and I looked at each other. Either we didn't know her as well as we thought we did or Jess was getting smarter by the hour.

Carly waved it off.

"Whatever it was, I didn't give much thought about what to call it. All I knew was that I was somewhere no one knew I was. Except for you guys no one was going to look for me, and I had to survive until I could get help."

"We didn't look for you," I admitted.

Jess started crying.

"We didn't know you were gone," Jess hiccupped.

"At least at first," I added. "When we stopped by your house you were never home. We thought the thing with Alden had taken off and you were spending all of your time with him."

"And Mr. Wiske had taken away your cell phone in gym class . . ." Jess reminded her, dabbing her eyes with the corner of her shirt.

". . . So there wasn't a way to call you. And you didn't answer the phone at your house," I finished.

Carly nodded. "I never got it back. Someone stole my phone out of his office."

"Likely story," Jess huffed in between sniffles, "He probably kept it for himself."

Even Jess knew this couldn't be true. Carly's phone was one of those cheap things you buy at the drug store and pay for as you go. She didn't have a phone plan since her parents were among the negative three percent of the population that didn't believe in cell phones. After they were killed by the drunk driver and the estate lawyer had put all the house bills on an electronic payment system that slurped money from the estate's account until Carly told him otherwise, she had been too depressed to replace even her cheap one.

"If it makes you feel better, Wiske left the summer after we graduated. I don't know if he moved to a better school or if he retired or what. But there's a new gym teacher now," Jess continued.

I interjected, "He married Tutti Huesner."

"Wait. Cutie Tutti?"

Jess and I nodded in agreement with Carly's unspoken thought. Marriage just out of high school wasn't unheard of where we lived, but it wasn't as usual as it had been, say, in the Middle Ages. Everyone had to admit, though, the flowers were gorgeous.

"And then I started getting letters every month telling me not to say anything about what happened in The Bagel Cafe or something would happen to you."

"And we didn't want anything bad to happen to you so we. Wait. What did we do again?"

Carly was leaning forward with her head in her hands and I'd started wishing I was back in my apartment with a cherry cola and two aspirin.

"We didn't do anything."

The minute I said it I could tell how horrible it sounded. Carly must think we were the worst friends to ever walk the Earth, and I would have to agree with her. It was just that at the time when it was all happening, doing nothing seemed like the right thing to do. I was the only one who was zoning out about the monthly letters, and they had started appearing when I was still out of town in college. Jess had gotten involved with Bobby buff and didn't know much about it until the night I told her about Carly's picture being sent with one of the letters. She hadn't known the extent of the puzzle in my mind until the day that Kent and Noah had come to The Flower Cart. Even then she didn't know about Carly's visit in the middle of the night or the man with the breath mint drugs until we were in Sarasota.

"We didn't know what to do."

It was the lamest excuse I had ever heard, and I was the one giving it.

Carly lifted her head up and shook it.

"I probably would've agreed with you. If you were told to keep quiet or I'd get hurt, what could you do? But it looks to me like you did do something anyway. I mean, why were you down in Florida?"

"It didn't have anything to do with minty drugs," Jess's words tripped over themselves.

That was great. One little request for her to not say anything about my being drugged and every time she opened her mouth it was the first thing that came out. She should've been the one getting the letters. This whole drama would've ended over a year ago because she would've been talking to everyone she saw. Except it probably would've meant something bad for Carly, so it was just as well that I was the one who was feeling like I'd messed up everything.

"What?"

"Never mind about that yet," I said, making a face at Jess which she knew full well was my 'I can't believe you said that' face.

"Tell us what happened then."

"Right. I wasn't a good kidnap victim. I fought them every way I could think of. I mean, I got punched pretty good, but I got some scratches in on them while they were at it."

"Wow. That doesn't even sound like you."

"I know. It wasn't. But I don't know. Something in me just boiled up and boiled over. I was thinking of my parents and my friends. I guess that's it. I probably wouldn't have fought for myself, but I would fight with everything in me for my parents and you guys."

At least one of the three of us fought when she should have instead of doing nothing.

"So I think they had planned to just kill me after they'd sold me those times those first months . . ."

I swerved onto the shoulder of the road, and we all got a scare from more than what Carly had just said. When I got back on track, she kept talking like nothing had happened. That's the good thing about friends: the silent agreement to keep on moving despite mistakes left and right or, in this case, onto the shoulder.

". . . but Mike talked them out of it. After I'd been in the shed for, like I said, maybe three months, they let me in the house more often."

"So you lived in the house then?"

"Only sometimes. Other times I was still locked in the shed. But when I was in the house, the guys there—there were about four of them—just started relaxing around me. At that point I didn't scratch unless I was hit. They were all bigger than me. I mean, what was I gonna do? Rip them apart with my bare hands?"

Jess snorted a laugh and water came out of her nose. Then the three of us laughed for awhile because it really was kind of funny. Plus the thing with Jess's nose brought us all back to the old days when we were less sophisticated. Laughter is a comfort sometimes and energizing at others. We needed something to laugh about.

"When it was just the four of them and me," Carly continued after she caught her breath, "it was kinda okay. There was another guy that stopped by sometimes. I think he was from the base operation. It was a family thing, I think. I don't know. But they put me in the shed when he was there. One time they didn't have time to and sent me upstairs. I cracked open the bedroom door and watched them with him. And I started doing little things, like cleaning up after them, maybe picking some wildflowers when they let me outside with a guard and putting them in a jar on the table, things like that. And they started thinking of me as not as much of a captive as at first." She paused, "Maybe more like a pet. Not an actual person, because if they did that they would have some real cognitive dissonance going on. . ."

I smiled at Carly's perfect phrase and Jess rolled her eyes.

". . . what with the way they trafficked the other . . ."

"What others?" Jess and I both asked.

"They mostly marketed drugs, but their business wasn't limited to that. They sold girls, too. Sometimes little boys. The ones they didn't sell, they rented out."

Jess's face took on an expression of horror even she wouldn't have believed had she been able to see herself.

Carly saw it, and finished, "They're awful, awful people, but it's a bigger business than the ones I was living with. Those guys were just a real small part of it. And I didn't see much of it at all. I just picked up snatches of conversation in addition to my own experience at first. That's how I know.

"Anyway, since they started thinking of me as more of a pet, I escaped some of the other stuff. And because of Mike."

"What were their names?" Jess asked.

"Besides Gunns and Mike it was Gemini and Dickie. I don't know last names, maybe not even real first names."

I snorted. "Because Gemini sounds real."

Carly snorted back.

"Sometimes I cooked a little. They always liked that. They liked chocolate chip cookies. I heard them talking one time about whether to have me deliver drugs, but they decided if someone recognized me it could blow their business, so they didn't."

Carly put her hands on each of our arms.

"I wouldn't have, you know. Even if they would've killed me, I wouldn't have done that. If someone who was drinking alcohol had killed my parents, why would I ever bring something like that to someone?"

We knew she was absolutely telling the truth.

"Then I started thinking more about it. I mean, until I could find a way to get out of there without anyone catching me, why didn't I find out what I could about what they were doing so I could bring some information to someone who could do something with it to stop them?"

"Wow."

Jess was impressed beyond words, but who wouldn't be?

I slowly shook my head. "That was really brave, Carly."

She laughed.

"Maybe. But it was selfish, too. I wasn't just thinking of my parents. I was thinking maybe if I did one great thing in my life that it would impress Alden."

We couldn't help but nod in agreement. Maybe by surviving she already had.

15

It was getting dark by the time Carly had filled us in on what we all began calling the prison plantation; plantation for short. We called it that because although she said it was just an ordinary house on a country road and there weren't any other buildings that she could see, there was a lot of land around it. Plus, plantation owners didn't have a good rep in our history class, so it seemed to fit. We took turns driving back and it wasn't as tiring this time because there was so much to talk about and because there were three of us taking turns driving instead of two. We didn't even stop to sleep in the car like last time and, fortunately for us, when we were in the grocery store that one day, I had bought a jumbo package of baby wipes that we used for sponge bathing once a day. I know. Sometimes I amaze even myself.

Even though I hadn't gotten any decent information from Trudy Tilden, we all agreed it was the work of the good Lord, Himself, that Jess and I were outside of Sarasota in the same parking lot as Carly and that the trip to Florida was the best thing we'd done so far.

See, according to Carly, Gunns and Mike had to drive a package down to Miami. Anyway, the guy from the base operation who stopped by sometimes had instructed them to bring Carly with them. They told her he said it would look more normal if they were seen with someone like Carly. Oh yea. Two guys with tattoos and scars would look much more innocent with someone like Carly sitting in the backseat.

They had taken a detour to drop something off at a warehouse in another town which had set them back a few hours, but they still thought they'd make the Miami delivery on time. The handles on the inside of the back doors had been removed, so the two of them must have figured she wouldn't be able to run without them catching her because they both went into the Burger Kwik. What they didn't know was that she'd seen my car when they were pulling into the lot and had decided her now or never moment had come. There's something to be said for keeping an old beater, and this was a big something. My bumper sticker that said "Friends don't let friends wear clogs" tipped her off, too. If I hadn't been driving ye olde rattletrap from high school and she hadn't recognized it, who knows what could have happened to her once they got to Miami?

There was one smart thing and one thing that we didn't know how to categorize that Carly had done when she saw us and before she got my attention so I could let her out of their car. One was to write a short note to Mike, telling him she hoped things went well in Miami and that life would be good to him and to not worry about her. She figured they had a deadline as far as their Miami delivery, so the note would give them both the reminder to keep moving and some kind of defense to the rest of the guys for leaving her when they got back. Plus, she really was grateful for Mike. If he hadn't been part of the group, she'd have been toast. And other than an irritating habit of burping really loud, he'd kind of grown on her. I wasn't about to bring up the Stockholm Syndrome thing. Whether she'd convinced them to trust her or vice versa wasn't at the top of our list of things to untangle just now.

The other thing she did was grab the title of the car from the glove compartment.

"You what?!" Jess screamed.

We were all a little loopy from reliving the last year and a half of Carly's life and her reaching into the front to get to the glove compartment right when she had her first and maybe only opportunity to escape seemed too risky or maybe downright crazy.

"Why didn't you just write down the license plate?" I asked.

"Look. If you guys want to be held captive by some pretty creepy guys for a year and a half and then think on your feet perfectly when you have your first chance for a big exit, be my guest."

"Sorry."

"Yea, sorry."

We'd gotten so caught up in Carly's account, that we'd forgotten all about the really crummy things that went with it like sadness and fear and disgust and anger and loneliness and not thinking clearly when you see a chance to escape.

Anyway, it was done now. We weren't exactly going to drive back to the Burger Kwik and return it.

We pulled into a gas station and switched drivers again. Jess and I had automatically taken to switching with either me driving or sitting in the backseat so I could hear what was being said.

"Patty, you don't have to be so nice. You can ride shotgun," Carly finally said.

"Um, no, I'm fine back here."

"No, really. Get up in front you sweet thing, you."

"Carly, she can't hear out of her left ear. If she's driving, she can hear what we're saying, but if she's in the passenger seat, she won't. She'd have to be turned halfway around to catch everything."

"What? I can't believe that. You two are kidding me."

I shook my head.

"It's true, Carly."

I pointed to the left side of my head. "Dead ear."

Carly leaned over and whispered something. I didn't hear a thing.

She straightened up.

"Really?"

"Really."

"Because you would have reacted to what I said. Do you want to know what I said?"

I shrugged. We needed to get back on the road instead of having a conversation about my hearing. I climbed into the back seat and Jess took the wheel.

"Was it a virus, Patty?!" Carly shouted.

"You don't have to shout, Carly. I can hear just fine out of my right ear."

"They say sometimes that happens with a virus, but sometimes your hearing can come back after that, too. I saw it on the news once. A lady lost her hearing when she was sick, but it came back later. Maybe it will come back."

I shook my head at Jess. I could tell she was getting ready to get into the whole gunfire thing that no one heard but me, but that would have taken us down another road entirely. There was no sense getting into everything that had happened at the Bagel Cafe the night of August 8th. If Carly wanted to believe my not being able to hear what she'd whispered in my left ear was because of a virus, she could for now. We had to lay out Carly's version of events first, kind of like putting together the edges of a puzzle before filling in the rest.

"Forget about it for now, okay? The thing I don't understand, Carly, is how you could've visited me in the middle of the night if you were trapped on prison plantation all that time."

It seemed like an innocent enough question, but Carly started hyperventilating and I rubbed her shoulders until she calmed down.

"I'm sorry," I said, "Never mind. It doesn't matter, does it Jess?"

Jess was shaking her head 'no' which made me a little nervous since she was at the wheel, and when she drives, the car moves whatever direction she's looking.

Carly started breathing normally again and ran her fingers through her hair.

"No, it's okay. Actually, that was probably riskier than this. There's no way those guys would know we're friends, so they couldn't have known that a party they went to one floor down was so close to a friend of mine. That was the only other time I got off the plantation. Gunns wanted to take me to show me off to some old pals of his. I was hoping he wouldn't rent me out like at first. But if they were into anything, it was probably drugs. They were just guys from when he was in high school. He told me to pretend I was his girlfriend. He even bought a new shirt for me to wear instead of the one I lived in at the plantation. Let me just say here and now, he has the dirtiest fingernails you've ever seen. And he sweats easily. Aaand he isn't real regular with his shower schedule."

"Gross!" Jess slapped the steering wheel.

"Oh you poor thing," I groaned.

"Mike had stayed in the car just to keep a look out for things. I don't know what they were looking out for, but every time they went somewhere, they went in pairs."

"It's probably part of the whole drug dealing thing," Jess said as though she worked for the DEA and had her ten year pin.

"They didn't deal, Jess, at least as far as I know. It was more like a delivery business."

I raised my eyebrows at Carly, but she didn't see me.

"When the party had been going on awhile, I told him I needed some fresh air. It was believable. In addition to some deep fried something that coated the whole apartment with the smell of grease, the smoke in that apartment could've killed a horse."

"I always wondered about that apartment," I said, squinting my eyes and frowning.

"That was when I slipped out and ran up to your apartment. I wanted to stay there, but if I had, it would've been only a matter of time before Gunns knocked down every door in the building looking for me. And then what would've happened to you?"

Jess was shaking her head back and forth again, only this time I joined her. If something had happened, I wouldn't have known what hit me because I was still out of it from the minty drugs.

"I can see why it's a bad memory," I offered.

Carly laughed, then frowned. "Oh it's a bad memory alright, but not for the reasons you're thinking. Earlier that day I'd heard them talking about something the guy from the base operation had given to one of the guys at a delivery point. Anyway, he'd said he picked up this list and, from what he said, it seemed important that it not get in the wrong hands. They talked about how maybe they should just shred it, but then thought they'd better let the guy make that decision. I didn't know what it might be for, but I just slipped it into my pocket when they were getting ready for the party. It was what I left on your T.V. when I visited you that night, Patty."

I was starting to get chills. Maybe it was because we'd driven north enough that the Florida sunshine was no longer our happy little companion, but I didn't think so.

"When we got back to the plantation, the place was torn apart. The other guys were yelling at each other about losing the list. I don't know why they didn't think of me, but they never did. It was a very long night."

We all sat in silence for a few minutes just thinking of Carly's bravery in coming to my apartment.

"So you took a chance just to see me?"

Carly huffed her disbelief at the self-centered question. I was immediately embarrassed I'd asked it. We were all coming at this from our own precious perspectives, though her experience trumped mine by a long shot. I took a little comfort that at least I'd had the drama of getting a letter every month from some mysterious source while Jess had no drama to claim except flirting with Bobby with mixed results.

"I thought maybe you knew how to get me out of there. I don't know. Like maybe you had some private detective hanging out at your apartment all the time trying to find me. And then—ta da—it would all be over. But you were sooo groggy. I tried to give you as much of an idea as I had, myself, about where they had me, but it didn't seem like you were getting it."

I looked out the window. I had botched things up completely. Not only was there no one watching for Carly to show up, but the police didn't exactly find me trustworthy or why would they keep questioning me? I didn't even remember her saying anything about where she was.

One thing I did have, though, was that slip of paper. I hadn't left it on a flat surface since that night. No one could get it if I kept it in my pocket, right? It had changed pockets from sweats to jeans depending on the day, but I always had it with me. I pulled the crumpled list out of my pocket now and passed it around. None of us could make heads or tails of it, but if it had caused such a ruckus at the plantation, it must be important enough to hold on to.

By the time we got back home there were still some unanswered questions, but we figured we could sort it out in a few days' time and then go down to the police station and talk to Noah Berkl. Maybe we'd even get lucky and see Mr. FBI tall, dark, and handsome Kent Damon.

Isn't it funny how just when you think you've got everything figured out, you don't?

16

By the time we got back, it was dark out. Part of the reason was because winter in the Midwest means feeling like it's time for supper at the same time you'd be ready for an afternoon swim during the summer. Another reason was that every time we stopped for a bathroom break we stocked up on more to drink. It wasn't just Jess either. It was a self-perpetuating cycle kind of like the water cycle you learn about in grade school. We couldn't help ourselves. If anyone had listened to us, they'd have thought they were in a field of bird-covered trees at suppertime. Just when one of us would say something the other one or two would chime in. We're good together that way. Anyway, our throats were in constant need of hydration due to the steady flow of chatter.

Somewhere in Iowa we'd decided Carly should to stay with me for awhile since we didn't know when Gunns and Mike would be back from Miami and figured they might already have someone watching her house. Jess didn't want to miss out on anything, so I ended up with Carly taking up space in my double bed and Jess sleeping on the couch. The first night we were so exhausted from the trip and everything that went with it, we pretty much fell asleep the minute we got everything out of the car and up to my apartment. Fortunately, we'd packed light. Carly didn't have anything but what she was wearing.

Since Jess had two vacation days left and I still had a day before I had to go back to The Flower Cart, we planned to take the next day to settle in and figure things out. Then we could go down to the police station and give the big reveal to Noah Berkl and (I hoped with all my might) Mr. Hunky guy of the FBI. Not only could I feel vindicated about my version of what happened at The Bagel Cafe, but Jess and Carly might even see Kent Damon whereupon the three of us could share knowing looks of agreement about his gorgeousness.

Carly was still drooling out of the side of her mouth when I woke up. She'd gone slack-jawed in her sleep as long as I could remember, even when we had sleepovers in third grade. I pulled back my side of the covers as quietly as I could. She deserved to sleep late. As far as I was concerned she deserved to sleep another straight week after all she'd been through, but it's doubtful she slept much more than a minute longer, since just when my feet hit the floor Jess started banging around in the kitchen like a raging rhino.

I tiptoe ran as fast as I could. Didn't she have a quiet bone in her body?

"Jessicaaa!" I whisper shouted.

Jess turned and I pointed to my bedroom as I put my finger to my lips.

She kept on slamming cupboard doors.

"Can't you stop it with the cherry cola already?" she said pointing to the refrigerator, "And what happened to the mint stuff? You always have mint stuff!"

She was pouring water in my coffee maker and I couldn't help but notice she measured an extra scoop of coffee into the filter. Okay, that was just plain mean. I'd gotten over my aversion to the bean that I'd acquired after the mint incident, but that didn't mean I could stand my coffee extra strong without having the memory of that crummy feeling crash over me again like waves before a tsunami. Jess was obviously in a mood.

"Maybe I've been out of town, Jess, like down to Sarasota. And maybe one of my best friends used it up last time she was here and I haven't had time to replace it. And maybe that friend should find it in her heart to be a little quieter since another friend is sleeping off bad memories of the last year and a half."

Jess poured some coffee, squeezed some caramel ice cream topping in it, and stirred. She took a sip while she held something in front of my face. It was the car title that Carly had grabbed before she switched from Gunn's car to mine in Sarasota. Jess must have picked it up from the pile of stuff we'd dumped by the door the night before.

"What?"

"The name. There? There. *There.*"

I grabbed the title from her and looked at it. Then I started at the top, reading every word just in case I was misunderstanding something. There were two names listed, and one was very familiar.

"Do you have some of that coffee for me?" Carly asked with a yawn.

She was standing in the entry way to the kitchen looking soft and snuggly. Jess and I turned and blinked at her for a full minute. It wasn't that we hadn't seen Carly with her hair tangled from sleep or even that we were surprised she was up what with all the noise from the kitchen. It was something more unsettling than either of those things.

"Help yourself," I said as I walked into the living room and slumped on the couch. Jess was right behind me.

"Now what?!" she whispered.

Jess's whispers, especially when she was tired, were very often more like quiet talking overlaid with a breathy sound, and she didn't seem to notice that the people she was trying to leave out of a conversation always had a pretty good idea about what she was whispering.

"Now what what?" Carly asked as she joined us in the living room.

What else were we going to do? Keeping secrets among the three of us had all the allure of fresh manure on a cornfield. I held up the title.

Carly reached for it, but Jess snatched it away.

"Would you mind telling us why your name is on the title of a car that the people who took you were driving? The ones who are drug dealers?"

"Delivery . . ." Carly reached for the title.

"Drug dealers!"

Jess being Jess, I knew she wouldn't hold back, but her volume level was sliding close to very loud.

I caught her eye and pointed to my entry door. There were other people living in this building besides me.

"There's no way my name is on there. Let me look at it."

I grabbed it from Jess and handed it to Carly who started studying it.

"On the line," Jess said.

Carly's face got a horrified look on it. It reminded me of the way werewolves in those really bad late night movies look before they change from being human.

"Why is my name on this car title? *How*?"

Jess was tapping her foot.

"Likely story. What happened? Did you and Mike actually have a thing going?"

A tear slipped from the corner of Carly's eye, and I handed Carly the box of Kleenex I kept for times like this; not that

I would have ever in a million years thought this particular time would take place.

"Come *on*, Jess," I said as I went to get the coffee pot.

It was going to be a long morning.

"Don't forget the caramel."

Jess could multi-task with the best of them.

"Did you decide, oh well, since I left my sweet little innocent *stupid* friends I might as well take my chances with these creepy muscle-bound dudes? They'll never know? Well now we *know*, Carly! Now we *know*!"

Jess was up and pacing in my living room. It was just a matter of time before we all got dizzy.

"I didn't know it was on here! Cross my heart!"

"Spit swear?" I asked.

Carly crossed her heart, spit on her fingers, and wiped them on my pajama sleeve.

Jess sat down next to Carly.

"I don't know, Carly. It looks pretty fishy."

"She just spit swore, Patty," Jess defended her as though Carly had just presented us with the Treaty of Versailles, which I'm thinking was something not everybody was happy with at that time either. At the moment, I was feeling a little like Germany.

At heart, Jess always had been (and I was here and now a witness to 'and will always be') a pushover. She had apparently forgotten that not a minute before she was ranting like a raving lunatic at the person on whose shoulder she was now resting her head. She went from raging rhino to little lamb in the blink of an eye.

"Okay, Patty. Don't trust the friend you've had since second grade: the one who let you practice braiding on her own hair even though it hurt ten ways 'til Sunday, the one who kept the secret about what happened at the YMCA pool, and the one who delivered that note to Peter St. Cloud during math class."

I closed my eyes and shook my head. We did have a history, after all.

"Why would I have grabbed the car title if I thought it would implicate *me* in this mess?"

"You have a point."

"What happened at the YMCA pool?" Jess asked, looking up curiously.

We both ignored her.

"I don't even know why I grabbed it."

I did a shimmy dance with my shoulders. It helped.

"Okay, fine. But how do you explain your name on here?"

I grabbed the title and waved it in the air.

"How should I know?"

"Yea, how should she know?"

How should any of us know? Bringing Carly to Noah Berkl and Kent Damon would make all kinds of sense except they didn't know about us being friends in the first place. What would they think if I brought her to them a year and a half after her disappearing from under the FBI's nose?

Considering the fact that they tended to be suspicious of me anyway, my suddenly producing a missing person wasn't exactly a way to alleviate their suspicions. They probably wouldn't believe the truth. After all, it wasn't very believable. No, it would look more like I was in on the drug thing than in on a rescue. And say they somehow miraculously did believe us. Now we had another problem that was even harder to explain. If I told them that there were some very bad guys who were driving a car I could describe by the very specific car title I produced, they would clearly see Carly's name on it, and there was nothing to prevent them from thinking that Carly had been in on it all along.

We had thought the whole thing would be over within a day or so of us getting back home. Then I could go back to living the dream that I didn't know I'd had as owner, president, and CEO of The Flower Cart; and Jess could go back to flirting with Bobby buff; and Carly could finally start living the life she'd planned to live after high school. But how was that going to happen when the only thing I had to identify one of Carly's dirty-fingernailed, sweaty, unwashed captors with was a government document implicating Carly?

We were all coming to the same conclusion. I could tell because we all talked at the same time. Jess said, "They'll put you in jail" and Carly said, "They'll arrest you" and I said, "Jess will be the only one free to figure it all out".

Carly and I sat with our heads in our hands and Jess went to the kitchen and rummaged around in the refrigerator.

17

"What can you tell me about the vacuum repair shop that was here before The Flower Cart?"

Francis gave me a confused look.

"I know. I didn't know it was here either," I said.

I slid the note from Trudy Tilden, the one that said *Bigger than it seems* on one side and *equipment* on the other, back into my pocket. Then I said out loud something that I often thought about, but that politeness had until now kept behind my lips.

"Ha ha ha, Patty, that's a good one."

It didn't take much for Francis to be entertained. I'd only said I wondered if Mrs. Baxtrom ever got tired of getting her dead husband's flowers. Before I could tell him that I wasn't joking, Melissa knocked quietly on the door jamb and came in. Her neck was starting to get blotchy. What now?

I'd been back at work for a week. The first day I was as jumpy as a puppy. After that first day, though, I'd gotten used to the idea of Jess, Carly, and me figuring more things out on our own. We'd even made a list: one, what happened at the Bagel Cafe; two, what Carly had seen that day in high school when she visited me at the fine establishment I now owned; three, how did Carly's name get on the car title; four, what did the list that Carly grabbed actually mean; and five, who all was involved in the delivery business? Yes. I said it. I'd started calling the drug dealing and trafficking a delivery thing instead and so had Jess. If we said it any other way, Carly would get upset and between the two of us, we'd decided Carly didn't need any more things in her life to upset her just now. I'd settled back into a routine of doing everything I had been doing for the past six or so months as The Flower Cart owner. The difference, of course, was that I was also keeping an eye out for the man with the mints plus trying to figure everything else out while I ran my business.

Melissa held up one hand to hide what she was doing with the other one, which was pointing toward the cooler. And here was number six: Noah Berkl and Kent Damon.

I sighed. Then I decided that ignoring their presence would give my heart time to stop thumping audibly and return to its normal pace. What those two men were doing looking at flowers through the glass doors was their business. Maybe Noah was thinking of getting something for his wife besides the usual bouquet he bought for her at the convenience store every anniversary. The things we tell ourselves to avoid the truth are many and varied.

"Melissa, can you write a sweet note to these three people and sign with the names there?"

I pointed, handing her the short list. Two were for anniversaries. Besides having nice handwriting, Melissa was great at coming up with sappy quotes and sappy closings to match. The other one was for a birthday.

"The bouquets are already done and in the cooler. Francis can help you get them out so you can insert the cards."

I turned my head.

"Francis, will you please . . ."

Francis was already shaking his head back and forth.

". . . put those three . . ."

He was edging toward the back door with his coffee.

". . . with your next delivery?"

"I like you, Patty, and I like my job, and don' get mad at me, but don' ask me to get stuff outa there now. Those two guys give me the funny look, you know?"

Oh I knew. Why else were the three of us huddled in my office?

Then I got mad. It wasn't right that I felt like a hostage in my own shop just because those two had walked through the door. I was an upstanding citizen whether they believed it or not. For all I knew maybe *they* were criminals posing as one very ordinary local policeman and one hunky FBI agent. The thought gave me a jolt of courage, kind of like I was at a WWE smack down. I didn't care what my face would look like at the end of it all! I was going in and taking them down! I stood up. Then I sat back down and lectured myself about thinking before speaking.

It didn't take much. As a girl, I had heard the lecture about as many times as there are dollars in the national debt. 'Once something is said, it can't be unsaid. You can back peddle or apologize or pretend you were misunderstood, but everyone who heard you say it will know differently. And forget about the whole "misspoke" expression. That is only for politicians who think people actually believe them when they say it.' Oh I heard it all word for word. I could even hear her voice. There was no one as good as my mother at putting a damper on things.

I left Francis and Melissa in the back room and walked over to the cooler.

"Excuse me, Noah."

I nodded to Kent as though I didn't remember his name or how gorgeous he was. I nearly lost my balance. Stunning men can do that to people like me. Poor Jess wouldn't have stood a chance.

I reached into the cooler, pulled out a bouquet, and handed it to Noah. He looked at me like I'd lost my mind.

"A little help?"

There was no reason to not take advantage of the situation. Noah took the bouquet because he didn't know what else to do and because he was used to being pushed around by his wife. I don't mean anything bad by that. I handed the other one to Kent, and grabbed the third.

"Just put them over there on the counter," I said nonchalantly.

I couldn't believe it. They actually did. I turned to them.

"What a surprise to see you here. Have you figured out what happened at the Bagel Cafe yet? I suppose you've been working night and day to sort it out since you have so much information from all of your interviews from nearly a year and a half."

I was trying to be friendly and slightly approachable, but I could feel my frustration frosting the edges of my words, and not in a cherry cream cheese way either, but in a gritty, icy tenth snowstorm of the winter way. Frustration will do that.

Kent spoke first.

"You closed your shop for a few days."

"Yes, I did—Kent is it?"

'Well played', I thought to myself.

The corners of Kent's mouth twitched slightly.

"It's Kent Damon, Patty."

Noah was trying to be helpful, apparently unaware that Kent Damon and I were having a stare down. I was trying to not get lost in his eyes that were the color of molten chocolate.

Noah tugged at the corner of his collar.

"Why did you close up shop for those days, Patty?" Noah asked.

"I needed a vacation."

"Where did you go?"

"I can't think of why that would be any of your business, Noah, but since you're interested, let's just say I went to Vegas with some friends."

I was pulling off a sophisticated lady persona pretty well if I do say so myself. I shook my hair to the side for good measure. However, I don't even know how that last sentence came out of my mouth. It just kind of flew out.

I've never been able to figure out if all lies are bad. For instance, telling someone they look nice when they really look fairly ordinary doesn't strike me as bad as someone cutting out the liver of a kitten and selling it for research and then denying it. Still, in this case I wasn't so sure I should've told one. Maybe this whole experience was pulling me to the dark side. Then I consoled myself with the thought that it wasn't really a lie. I hadn't said I went to Vegas, had I? I said 'let's just *say* I went to Vegas'. It made me feel much better.

The bell on the door jingled just then as Mrs. Baxtrom came in. I had never been so glad to see her in my life.

"Mrs. Baxtrom!"

I walked toward her as though I was seeing my best friend.

"Patty," Mrs. Baxtrom tittered with her worn-out smoker's voice, "I'm glad you missed me. I've been down in my vacation home for a short break from the cold."

"Vacation home?"

"Yes, of course. Ah, the palms. I'm partial to the foxtail."

I had no idea what she meant, but nodded knowingly.

"The warmth is so nice down there."

My luck was holding. Mrs. Baxtrom was actually talking to me before ordering me around.

"And where is that?"

"Key Biscayne. It was relaxing," Mrs. Baxtrom suddenly arched her eyebrows, "but there's a flower show coming up in two weeks. They'll need my advice, of course."

The Mrs. Baxtrom we all knew and feared was back. She started placing a few orders as Noah and Kent walked out the door. Melissa slipped the cards she'd been writing into the bouquets on the counter, and Francis carried them out to his truck. I wouldn't be seeing any more of him today.

It was close to closing time, so I told Melissa she could go home. I was cashing out the register when it hit me. Noah and Kent hadn't asked to see me. Sure, they'd asked me about my closing up shop for a short break, but they didn't drill me with twenty questions like the other time. I was the one who had approached them. I had come out of my office to see them, and they had been looking in the cooler.

I walked over to the cooler and looked at it. The man with the mints had examined it, too. He had run his fingers up and down the edges of it the day he came in and knocked on the walls before knocking me out with the mints in the tin in his pocket lint.

Back in the days when the years had three numbers in them instead of four, someone named Ambrose said something that people quote sometimes. I don't remember exactly what he said because at the time the teacher was telling us about it someone threw a pencil, and it landed on the desk of the girl beside me. It was probably in Latin, so I wouldn't have understood it anyway. But whatever it was that he said, it meant when you're in a certain place just act like the people around you are acting and it will make your visit go more smoothly. Anyway, there weren't any people around me to copy, and since the store belonged to me, I was the one who should be the copy-ee, not the copy-er. But I was in way over my head as far as strangers and semi-strangers were concerned, so when in Rome, right? I ran my fingers over the edges of the cooler. The gaskets appeared to be just like they always seemed: happy to do their boring job sealing the cooler air from the rest of my musky shop. I opened the door and leaned in. I lifted every vase and container and looked in them and under them. I pressed on the sides and the back. I succeeded only in getting some baby's breath caught in my hair and breaking a small white vase.

Great. I'd have to clean up this mess before I could leave for the day. At least I fit in with the others who had looked at the cooler because I'd come up with nada just like they had. Score one for Ambrose.

I rummaged through a corner of the backroom, returned to the main part of The Flower Cart with ye olde vacuum cleaner we used once a week, and vacuumed up the tiny bits of glass that were too small to pick up with my fingers. The cooler wasn't as cold as I remembered it being when I worked for Trudy in high school. Dinosaur that it was, that wasn't really a surprise. Yet I had to admit I hadn't cleaned the coils even once since I'd bought the place.

I'd never investigated the cost of floral display coolers, but it wasn't hard to guess they would probably cost more than my miniscule savings could even begin to touch. Even if business at The Flower Cart took off the way it did after Tutti Huesner's wedding to the gym teacher, who knew how many flowers I'd have to sell to afford it? Plus, who wanted that much work on their hands? I had enough going on with everything else at the moment.

I switched off the power to the cooler, got down on my hands and knees, and unscrewed the grill, sending it clattering loudly to the floor. Then I sneezed. It's amazing how much dust can accumulate when you leave it alone for awhile.

I left on the attachment, switched on the vacuum again, and began sucking up the dirt and dust that had accumulated over the time Trudy had been gone. There was a lot of grit. A lot. How did the cooler keep on working at all? Then I stopped. Something was in the way. I bent my head and peered into the darkness but couldn't make anything out. I dusted myself off and jogged back to my office to pull a flashlight out of my desk drawer, mumbling 'Please, please, please don't let it be a dead mouse' under my breath.

This was becoming a much bigger project than I'd intended when I first stuck my head in the cooler.

By now Jess and Carly would both be wondering where I was. Since our trip to Sarasota, we were all conscious now of who was out of my apartment and for how long. This couldn't take much longer, though, and the thought of a dead something awaiting its heavenly home under my flower cooler was sure to keep me awake at night unless I bit the bullet, so to speak, and took care of it now. I peered through the darkness as I shined the flashlight over the base of the cooler. It sure didn't look like a mouse. It looked much worse. I shoved the flashlight farther back and leaned my forehead against the bottom edge. Then I sat back up and stared into space.

I jumped up and checked the doors to make sure they were locked. I looked into the base of the cooler again and reached back to the things that were blocking the vacuum from slurping up all the dust. Then I began to count.

18

I shouldn't have worried about Carly and Jess wondering where I was because when I got home they weren't there.

We had agreed that Carly should stay put just in case someone saw her and recognized her. I use the term "agreed" loosely. Jess was of the mind that Carly had been out of town long enough that no one would be looking for her and that the guys she stayed with on the plantation were far enough out of town that they probably wouldn't be anywhere nearby. Carly was anxious to get to the bottom of who was involved in grabbing her out of her one in a million chance of a date with Alden and bringing them to justice. I, on the other hand, believed that once she got away there was no way in the world she should put herself within reach, visual or otherwise, of anyone who had even a remote chance of recognizing her.

When you have to watch out for both the good guys and the bad guys it doesn't leave much wiggle room for taking chances. After an extended conversation including pacing and grapes and cream cheese dip, they finally agreed with me. Score one for the paranoid crowd. So where was she?

There was any number of places Jess could be. She was catching up on the classes she was taking at the community college and working part time making persuasive sales calls to rich women, in addition to renewing her relationship with Bobby buff. Her brief absence had made his heart grow fonder, and Jess was beginning to mention his name in every other sentence with something that sounded like a coo every time she said it. Carly found it amusing, but that was because she hadn't lived with it as long as I had. I was beginning to think quietly to myself that if Bobby buff was a carton of milk, he would be sour and chunky by now.

Carly spent her time diagramming everything she could think of. It was her way of making sense of an experience that didn't make sense. I wondered if it was also her way to keep from going crazy with rage or depression, or some other very uncomfortable feeling, but if it was, she didn't say. She had diagrammed the layout of the house she had stayed in. She had sketched a map of the layout of the land around it, though there wasn't much information there. Lately she was making something that looked like a family tree using the names of the guys who had kept her locked up and any visitors she had known about or guessed about. She wrote the names of any girls or boys she had even an inkling of being trafficked, although she wasn't sure if they were the real names. She didn't have many of those, since it was only at the very beginning of her being there that she'd seen them or heard their names. She wasn't trafficked ("rented out" in her words) after Mike had convinced them it wasn't worth it to either traffic her or kill her; so she didn't catch glimpses of others like she had at first.

Every day she had sat in the same spot on the couch with her feet on the coffee table and a notebook in her lap. That meant that she should have been where I left her when I left this morning: in my apartment.

I sat down and waited. When I put my feet up on the coffee table, I noticed it had something sticky on it, so I grabbed a washcloth from the kitchen and gave the table a good cleaning. After putting the cloth in the hamper, I paced. I sat down again and ran my thumbnail over the fatty part my opposite index finger . Where was Carly?

Carly, Carly, Carly. Every day she had something to show the two of us. She was the one who, if not discovering anything new, at least was making a record the three of us could use as a reference point. Jess had contributed by buying more coffee and mint stuff to put in it. And also whipped cream, which, let's admit, no kitchen should be without. I finally had something to tell them and they were a no show.

I got up and looked out the window, but it had grown too dark to see anything. Leaving to look for Carly would only ensure all of us were gone at the same time just like it was before I got home, which is to say it would accomplish nothing.

I put a frozen pizza in the oven and pulled out the letters I'd gotten telling me to not say anything about what I'd seen at the Bagel Cafe. There was no reason to keep them behind my pizza pan any longer. I placed the box I kept them in on the coffee table in front of my couch. Maybe Carly would be able to figure out who was sending them if I showed them to her when she got home. If she got home.

I didn't have to think about it much longer. Just as the crusty, cheesy smell of a baked frozen pizza permeated the apartment, Carly and Jess both walked in.

"Mmm, what's that smell?" Jess made a beeline for the kitchen. What a surprise.

"Where have you been?"

"You don't have to sound like my mother."

The minute she said it, Carly's mouth turned down and her eyes got a little misty. She pulled her arms out of a navy sweatshirt that looked suspiciously like my hoodie. It went quite well with Jess's jeans and my shirt.

"I had something to check on and figured that if I wore a hoodie and pulled the hood up to cover my face like they do on the T.V. shows when someone doesn't want to be identified I could go wherever I wanted."

"Did it work?"

"I'm not sure. I think maybe. I have the stuff in the front pocket here."

"No. The hoodie. Did it keep anyone from recognizing you?"

"Um, yes?"

"Exactly. How do you even know if someone knows who you are or not when you're tripping down the street like Mary Poppins?"

"Mary Poppins in a hoodie," she sang.

"I have something to tell you guys."

Jess interrupted me. "For your dining pleasure!"

She brought in a tray of pizza slices and plates. I got up and came back with three cherry colas. Jess glared at me while Carly popped the top of her pop can. By now she had caught on to the thing Jess had about cherry cola. Sure, Jess had drunk cherry cola the night she first saw Kent Damon, but that was because she was so distracted she couldn't help herself. She hadn't touched it since.

"Let it go, Jess. If I can live at the plantation for over a year, you can get past one night at the Bagel Cafe. Besides, remember how much you used to love cherry cola?"

Clearly their minds weren't focused on much more than their appetites, so I'd have to wait another minute to tell them about Noah and Kent and my cleaning adventure. First things first. I slurped from my can just to back up Carly's point.

Carly held out a can to Jess and cocked her head.

I took another slurp and said, "We're here for you, Jess."

Jess looked from Carly to me to Carly and down to the can. She took it and popped the tab. We cheered. If Jess could drink a cherry cola without bolting from the room it would be quite an accomplishment in overcoming August 8th. Only sixteen hundred more items to go.

"I hasomding to tellu."

It's hard to talk with your mouth full, but I did the best I could. Apparently it wasn't as understandable as I thought.

Carly wiped her mouth with the sleeve of my shirt she was wearing.

"I was sitting here, you know, thinking about the guys and Gunns and Mike and why my name was on the title of the car. And I was thinking . . ."

"Oops! Pardonay mio. I didn't mean to drop that on the carpet."

I got up, grabbed the washcloth from the hamper to blot up the grease on my carpet, and lobbed it onto Jess's lap.

". . . why would someone put somebody else's name on a title? I mean, my name isn't the only one there, so I guess ownership wouldn't be in question, but it *is* on it."

"Why?" I gave up sharing my news and began to hum. Sometimes it helps the thinking process, and unlike Trudy Tilden I stayed on key.

"Take a tiny sip, Jess," Carly encouraged.

Jess took a tiny sip. I applauded and continued to hum.

Carly lifted the lid off my box of letters and frowned slightly.

"They wanted it to look like two people owned it?"

Carly made a face and tilted her head, while I started humming again.

"It was as close to an actual relationship with you as Mike could get?"

Carly rolled her eyes, and put the lid back on my box of letters.

"I have no idea."

"Neither did I, and I thought maybe if I had a change of scenery something would click. The best place for that would be my own house, right?"

"Well, no. The best place would be right here where no one can see you, so . . ."

"What about if they stole the car and wanted to shift the blame?" Jess asked as she took another sip.

We understood. Trying to overcome her anxiety associated with cherry cola and keeping up with our conversation was asking a lot. Maybe Carly and I had moved on to Carly leaving the apartment, but Jess still had her on the couch with her "family" tree and thinking about the car title problem.

"But one of the other guys' names was on it, too, Jess. He wouldn't have his name on it if it was stolen. It wasn't stolen, was it, Carly?"

I took the last bite of my pizza.

"I don't know. If his name was on it, it doesn't seem like it was. Let me finish."

Obviously Carly had gotten out of the habit of being interrupted, which was our favorite way of carrying on a conversation. Jess and I nodded to each other. She'd get over it, and we could deal with it for now. Baby steps.

"So I went to my house—I had the hoodie up the whole time I was outside, Patty—to just sit. I miss my house, plus, like I said, I thought it might help me think, even if I just sat in the backyard. And I took your letter opener with me in case I could use it to jimmy a window or something."

"Oh poor you," Jess said. "I bet it was good to go back."

Carly nodded.

"It was. And I went to the backdoor—the lock isn't great back there—and after a little pricking with your letter opener, Patty, and a bobby pin, it opened."

Carly's intake of breath was audible. "I could tell someone had been there. The walk in the back was icy and sloppy—it hadn't been shoveled after the last snow—but it looked like someone had walked on it. There were dirty dishes in the sink. The place smelled a little. And the wastebasket was full."

"Eww." Jess made a face.

I leaned forward.

"Who do you think it was?"

Carly let out a loud sigh.

"It had to be the plantation boys. Maybe not Mike . . ."

"Seriously. Are you sweet on him?" Jess asked.

I guess it had to be asked.

"No!" Carly raised her voice, "and stop interrupting me."

"How do you know it was them?"

I tried to interrupt in a nice way. We didn't need Carly getting all worked up in addition to Jess relearning to drink cherry cola.

"I don't know who else it could be. I mean there has to be some sort of limit on people who could break into my house, doesn't there? They took my purse that first night. Maybe they found my house key when they took it. So that would give them a way to get into my house."

Jess looked like she could live with that theory and I figured I could, too.

"Those rats! Were there tire tracks on the driveway?"

Carly shook her head.

"I didn't notice any. But I did find some things in the wastebasket."

"Time for another sip, Jess."

She was ignoring her cherry cola, and it seemed kind of important that we not let her. Sometimes if you can overcome the little things, it makes you feel like the bigger things aren't the size of Mount Everest.

Carly walked over and pulled out a bunch of papers she'd stuffed in my hoodie pocket and spread them out on the table.

"See? Here's some insurance updates on the car they were driving."

"Insurance?"

"Yea. And mailed to my name and my house."

When someone does something bad—for instance, if they kidnap someone—you don't usually think of them being concerned about obeying any other law. Yet, if Carly's money paid for car insurance, that meant they could stay legit and not have to pay for it.

"They must've somehow figured out how to contact my estate lawyer and include it with the other bills paid electronically."

"Creepy."

"And since your name is on the title it wouldn't make any difference to the lawyer."

"Tacky. Not only they steal you, but they steal your money for car insurance."

Carly was shaking her head. "Even if they found out who he was, I don't think a lawyer would consent to putting a name on this title without the consent of the owner which appears to be . . ." she looked at it closely, "me."

"At least we have a real name." I pointed to the other name on the title. "Besides Mike's, I mean."

Carly stiffened. "Wait. Back up. How would they know who my parents' estate lawyer is?"

We all looked at each other. How indeed?

"Is it possible he's part of the group?"

Jess and Carly stared at me. "You know. The plantation group? Or the, ahem, delivery business? Or . . . or . . . or something?"

"Not nice, Patty," Jess scolded, "A respectable lawyer?"

"Well?"

"Huh," Carly bit her thumbnail.

"Hey!" Jess jumped up, spilling some of her cherry Coke. "What if it was a gift?"

I drew a blank and it appeared Carly did, too.

Jess persisted. "What if your parents bought the car as a grad present before they . . . before they . . ."

Carly's face crumpled, but she nodded.

"Possibility?" I asked.

Carly nodded again. "They," she hiccupped, "had teased me about a graduation gift they were going to give me. At the time I thought it would be a real cell phone, not the disposable one I had."

Jess put in, "I still think Mr. Wiske kept it."

"I wonder if *he's* in on it?"

Carly slammed her pop can on the coffee table and threw it across the room.

"What?" I persisted, "I mean as long as we have the plantation boys plus who knows who else is part of the delivery business, and Carly's parents' estate lawyer, who's to say someone at the high school isn't involved? Maybe that's why he left."

I was beginning to get a headache, but Carly was the one who started rubbing her temples.

"Maybe my parents had put the car in my name and were storing it somewhere."

"The estate lawyer would know where," Jess said darkly.

We sat silently, lost in our own thoughts. How much of a web was this thing? One thought I wouldn't share in a million years was one Carly broke the silence with.

"What if it wasn't an accident?"

"Your folks? It was a drunk driver, Carly," Jess replied.

"Maybe." It was clear from the way she said it, this wasn't the first time Carly had thought such a thing.

"But why would they arrange to kill your parents?" I said it because the can of worms was already partially opened.

None of us had an answer that didn't border on the world of mafiosos and someone named Gino. And, really, in our little town such a thing was a complete mismatch, so we reverted to discussing more solid ground. I know, I know. Our little town was starting to look like anything but the innocent patchwork of houses and people we'd grown up believing it to be. Even Jess's comment about 'a respectable lawyer' sounded unbelievable at this point. But when you've grown up believing one thing all your life, taking a turn, and, in this case, a pretty sharp turn, caused more than a little indigestion. And sometimes it's just easier to ignore what's new and run back to the familiar. Right and easy don't necessarily go together.

"How much did you look around, Carly? Was there anything else?"

"I went into every room except the basement. The area over by the furnace is always so cobwebby. I just kind of, I don't know, wandered, you know?"

Carly sighed and was quiet for awhile.

"I was just remembering how things used to be. Anyway, I went up and laid on my bed and pretended I was back in high school. I was remembering the fun we all used to have. Mmm. I could almost smell my mom's brownies.

"Then I looked through my drawers a little. I miss my clothes."

Jess was nodding her head sympathetically and I stared at the floor.

"There wasn't any way to carry my clothes, at least without being noticed walking down the street. I'd like to go back."

Carly finished filling us in on what she'd found at her house, and we finished the pizza. She was starting to leave long pauses in between her sentences and her eyes were droopy. We were all pretty tired.

I needed my friends' full attention when I told them about my day, but I wouldn't have it tonight. My information would have to wait until the morning.

19

Fortunately, the next day was Saturday and I only had to work ten to noon. I was home before Carly was even up. Jess walked in before I'd taken off my coat.

I raised my eyebrows at her.

"Scones with Bobby."

"What is it with scones?"

Jess shrugged.

"He likes scones. I don't know."

Her voice had lost its coo.

"Is something wrong?"

Jess shrugged. The day was getting off to a delightful start.

After she poured herself coffee in a very large cup that's meant for soup, she wandered over to the windows and looked out.

"Do you want to find an apartment together?"

I looked around to see if there was someone else she could be talking to.

"Um . . ."

"Because let's face it, this isn't the Taj Mahal you have here, and my apartment isn't much better."

"So we should move from two one bedroom apartments with threadbare carpet to one two bedroom apartment with threadbare carpet?"

"Maybe we could find a three bedroom."

I squinted.

"Carly has a house, Jess, just not one she can move back to right now without someone finding her and maybe taking her again. Or worse."

Jess turned from the window and sat down next to me on the couch.

"Bobby invited me to his house today. I'd never been there before."

"Woohoo?"

I honestly wasn't sure if I should be happy and excited or concerned and supportive. Jess's voice didn't match her words.

"It was really something. It even has a swimming pool."

Jess's voice was growing louder.

"Who would want a swimming pool here? You can use it like what? Two months out of the year? How stupid is that?!"

"Um . . ."

"And another thing. Those jeans he wears, the ones that cost three figures, they're, they're just stupid. And that car he drives around like some big man on campus. It's the stupidest car ever. "

Jess had a new favorite word of the day.

Carly was up, dressed, and joined us with her bowl of cereal. We hadn't even heard her.

Jess slurped down the rest of her minty coffee and went to the refrigerator.

"Want one?" she called.

"Um, okay?"

She returned with a bag of chips and three cherry colas.

The look on Carly's face would have had me in stitches any other time, but just now it seemed dangerous to laugh.

I opened my pop and took a sip.

Jess gulped hers and sat back like a man in a sweat-stained t-shirt and boxer shorts.

"Hm," she said.

Carly looked all kinds of questions at me and I shrugged back.

"She wants to get an apartment together," I whispered.

"That doesn't seem like it should cause such intensity. Though with Jess . . ." Carly's whisper drifted off as Jess leaned forward and took another long drink.

Carly and I stared while she finished the can.

Jess burped as she threw the can away and went to get another one. While we were glad for Jess's accomplishment, her sudden defiant attitude scared us a little.

She came back with another cherry cola and a plate of oatmeal cookies.

"You wanted to go back to your house?" Jess looked at Carly questioningly.

"Yea, but it's not an emergency. It doesn't have to be today."

Carly's voice sounded apologetic. She didn't need to apologize, but, at least in the past, with Carly, apologizing was an automatic reaction to crabby people.

"I think we should stake the place out, you know?" I suggested. "Like drive over there and sit in the car a few hours to see if anyone goes in or out. Then we'd know for sure who it was that had gone in there before."

I really thought it was a pretty decent idea and Carly nodded her head a little.

"I'm not sure we need to do that."

Jess pulled something out of her pocket and began playing with it.

I ran my fingers through my hair. Enough was enough.

"Jess, we can't read your mind. At least this time. First you come in here shrugging off your breakfast of scones with Bobby buff. Then you ask if I want to move and get an apartment together. Then you start complaining about swimming pools and expensive jeans!"

We didn't need to say anything about the cherry colas she was chugging like there was no tomorrow. There was no sense in admitting we'd created a monster.

Jess looked straight ahead, like she was the main character in a drama at the pinnacle of its big moment. She shook her hair once, closed her eyes, then she looked at us.

"As I said, Bobby showed me his house this morning. It was kind of a big deal. In all this time he's always taken me other places, never to his place. Then today when we met up in the college parking lot like usual, he asked if I wanted to hang out at his house. I thought, okay, he's in love with me, you know?"

"I bet you were dying," I said.

Even though I was tired of hearing about Bobby buff, Jess had fallen pretty hard for him. I had to be happy for her, at least in the moment.

"Dying. Like this is what I've been waiting for, right?"

It was. We were right there with her.

"His house was, well let's just say it was amazing. It was beyond what I would have ever thought he lived in. It gave me goose bumps.

We hung out awhile, drank some cocoa."

She leaned forward and grabbed my hand.

"With mint," she added like such a thing showed how truly wonderful he was.

"While he was showing me his home theater, I told him I was surprised by how nice his home was and he nodded like he knew I was surprised and was glad I was surprised and everything. Then he told me he was building a property management business, and that's why he was taking some college classes—you know, to bump up cred in the real estate market and maybe he'll be a real estate mogul one day and would I like to see some of his places. And I said 'okay', right?"

We nodded and kept nodding.

"So we drive around town and he points to some small house he says he's renting out to somebody. Then we drive around some more and here's one and there's one.

"Then we drive out of town by the place we had scones," Jess looked at me, "when we went to that antique mall that one day."

"When was that?" Carly asked.

"Before Florida. Doesn't matter. Go on, Jess."

"And we start to slow down, but then whiz by a nothing house, beige, right?"

Carly and I stopped nodding.

"He had started to say something, but then he stopped and didn't say anything. And I think 'no way', I'm just making things up in my head."

We started nodding again.

"So we're on our way back to his mega house when we drive by Carly's house and he says something about it being his next venture, but he doesn't quite have it yet."

Carly jumped up.

"What?!"

"I know, Carly, I know! And I think 'what!', right, but I'm all quiet and stuff. And I'm thinking 'oh no, oh no', you know? And then I think maybe I just thought he meant your house. Maybe it was the house next door."

"Sullbergers? They're retired. They wouldn't sell I don't think. Carters just bought the other side not that long ago. I wouldn't think . . ."

"Well how am I supposed to know?!"

"Are you sure it was Carly's? Maybe it just looked like Carly's."

"I think I know where my own friends live, Patty. It was Carly's! It was Carly's house! It even had the dent in the mailbox I put there when I pulled up too close that one time!

"And besides," Jess held up the thing from her pocket she'd be turning over in her hands, "I have his key to her house."

Carly and I both gasped at the same time.

"At least, I *think* it's the key to her house. When we got back I saw him drop a few keys in with another bunch of keys in the drawer of the side table in his entryway. They're labeled with addresses."

Jess dangled it in front of us.

"This," she said, "was an address I recognized."

Carly grabbed it and examined it.

"Does he know you took it?"

Jess shook her head.

"He thought I was in the bathroom."

By this time I'd gotten up and started pacing because Jess's morning had taken a turn worse than the one on the roller coaster at the fairgrounds; the one mothers don't want their children to ride because it's so old and one ride away from being a front page catastrophe on the evening news. Jess had eaten half the plate of oatmeal cookies, and Carly had picked up her notebook and started working on her diagrams. Only when she tossed it on the table, it wasn't a diagram. It was a sketch of a man's face.

20

I didn't get more than half a glimpse before Jess grabbed it.

"How do you know what Bobby looks like?"

Carly's eyes grew bigger than I'd ever seen them.

"What? I don't. That's the man who came to the plantation sometimes; the one who told Gunns and Mike and the others what to do. It's just—while you were talking about your morning with Bobby buff, for some reason he kept popping into my head."

Tears started forming in the corners of Jess's eyes and spilling over. I'd only every heard Jess talk about Bobby buff. I'd never met him, which at first I kind of understood and was slightly grateful for. By now, though? I should've met him by now. It's just that every time they went somewhere, he'd picked her up at her apartment or she met him somewhere, usually the college parking lot. Their dates never included friends. Neither of us thought anything of it. Lack of life experience does that to you. The one time Jess had asked if we could get together so he could meet her friend, he'd had something else come up. Little did he know he might have actually already met her friend. Only *that* friend was being kept hostage by some guys he told what to do. My stomach turned over.

I leaned over to get a better look. The minute I did, my mouth went dry. Oh man.

"Patty, you look like you've seen a ghost."

Even Jess dabbed her eyes long enough to look over at me.

I pointed to the drawing.

"The man. With the mints."

Jess's knee started jiggling up and down like a jackhammer.

"Enough about mints. You guys keep mentioning mints or minty drugs, and I have no idea what you're talking about."

Jess leaned back and covered her face with her hand. I filled Carly in about my morning at The Flower Cart and the strange customer who tapped on the walls and left a tin of expensive breath mints on the counter along with paper clips and pocket lint and how, not being one to waste anything, I had put the paper clips in my desk drawer and had eaten one of the breath mints and it knocked me out.

"So you were drugged?"

"Indubitably."

Okay, I just have to say this. Don't you love that word? My science professor used to use it to describe the theory of evolution. He didn't seem to think that something being without doubt *and* a hypothesis were mutually exclusive. I wish he would've thought the same way about giving me a good grade despite my test scores.

"And the effects were still wearing off the night you came to visit me during the party with Gunns."

Jess flopped over, hid her face in a throw pillow, and began quietly sobbing. It was okay. If her mascara left a smear on it, it would just remind me even more that it was she who had given it to me to celebrate my getting an apartment. The pillow was all flowery and stuff which fit Jess perfectly and stuck out like orange on red with my decor which wasn't decor at all, but more like secondhand cheap stuff.

"Wait. Jess, think."

I was asking a lot, considering Jess was in the middle of the worst nightmare of her life.

"Did you ever point to my apartment—like 'oh that's where my friend lives'—anything like that?"

"So he knows where you live." Carly started taking notes. Someone had to, or we'd end up going all sorts of wrong directions.

Tears still streaming, Jess pointed to what Carly had just written.

"Scratch that. I never did. He didn't seem interested in anyone else in my life. Ever. Not my family. Not my friends."

We waited a few minutes while Jess's crying alternated between wails and hicuppy jags.

"Our conversations never really scratched any sort of surface. I..I..I haven't even talked with him about the night at The Bagel Cafe. Can you believe it? When we were together it was just him and me. Me and him in a little bubble of love."

Normally there would have been a cooing sound at the end of that last sentence, but there was only silence.

Finally she said, "I am so done with that guy."

Jess said it too quietly. It was almost as if there was a volcano ready to erupt underneath her words.

We sat there together for awhile, each of us allowing our thoughts to wander all over the place. Finally I said what I hated to say, but had to be said.

"You can't break up with him."

Carly and Jess looked at me like I was insane.

I held up my hands.

"Just hear me out. Bobby buff still thinks Jess is gaga over him, even to the point of bringing you," I looked pointedly at Jess, "to his house today. If you're still his girlfriend . . ."

"Never!"

"Okay, his fake girlfriend that he doesn't know is fake, you can still get information from him."

Jess looked at me like I was asking her to pull out her fingernails.

"Right?"

Silence.

Carly got up and gave Jess a long hug.

"Just think about it for now, Jess, okay?" I said.

Jess shrugged.

"If this was a football game we would be losing from the time the starter gun went off."

"That's for races, I think," Carly interjected.

"Whatever. We have to go on the offense with this. We can't keep being surprised by the next thing. We've got to do a better job at figuring this out. Better than Noah. Better than Kent Damon. Better than Alden or Sam, though—where are they in all this?"

Carly and Jess shrugged.

"Who's with me?" My voice grew louder, "Who's with me?!!"

Carly and Jess just sat there and looked at me. I zoned in on Carly.

"So you want to get kidnapped again? So you want somebody to waltz in and steal your house like they're stealing your money for their car insurance?"

I shifted my gaze to Jess.

"So you want Bobby buff to keep leading you around like a puppet? You want to keep waiting for Gaston to turn into Prince Charming?

"I'll tell you one thing! I don't want to keep being questioned about The Bagel Cafe like I'm some sort of criminal. I'm already paying for that night with a dead ear! I'm done paying! I'll ask you one more time. With or without you, I'm going to get to the end of this. Are! You! With! Me?!"

Carly and Jess jumped up and pumped their fists in the air.

"Yeh!"

Carly apparently couldn't think of anything else to say in our moment of confusion and exuberance. But Jess could. She shook off the oppression of the morning's discovery and we began to feel the earth move.

"Heck yeh. He wants to play games with his little cuddly kitty?!"

We didn't really want to hear nicknames.

"He wants his sweet little cinnamon chipmunk to idolize those buff muscles like he's Batman or something?!"

We had to let her get it out of her system.

"He thinks he can do what he pleases and do whatever illegal things he wants and keep his cherry cheesecake cookie snookums in the dark?!!"

Jess pounded on the end table so hard it made her hand red.

"He's got another thing coming!!!"

We were pretty psyched with ourselves, but detailed plans weren't really our forte. Jess's knee started jiggling again. I stared into space trying to think of what to do. Carly turned to a new page in the notebook.

"What's first?"

"Hm," Jess squinted her eyes, "We need to figure out about the plantation and The Flower Cart and The Bagel Cafe. I mean, those are the places that have answers to the questions we have, right?"

"Leave my shop out of it."

"The Flower Cart is the place where I saw something I wasn't supposed to see," Carly reminded me, not that any of us had forgotten. It was like a feral hippopotamus following us around.

Jess added, "You thought something was weird, yourself, Patty. That's why you wanted to ask Trudy Tilden why she sold it to you so fast."

She was right, of course. Carly had seen something she wasn't supposed to see, and something happened that made Trudy sell her business, and they both had happened at The Flower Cart. I just hated the thought of the dream I didn't know I'd had being part of the mess we were trying to untangle.

I started nodding and my head wouldn't stop. I just kept nodding and nodding, like a bobble head.

"It started with a sudden decision by Trudy Tilden, Jess. She was straightening up the shop and stacking the mail when she asked me if I wanted to buy The Flower Cart. At the time it seemed kind of funny, but it all just happened so fast. One day I was her employee and the next day I was the owner and Trudy Tilden had moved to an address that didn't exist."

"So you think there's something fishy about The Flower Cart?"

Jess grabbed another oatmeal cookie and gave one to me. Wonderful. Now she wasn't just eating her stress away, she wanted me to help.

I laid the cookie on the table and put my head in my hands.

"Wait," Carly said, "Are you saying that there's more to the store . . ."

"The Flower Cart."

"The Flower Cart than my seeing something there? Like, like . . . like what?"

"Maybe the plantation guys use it for a meeting place!" Jess shouted, spitting a cookie crumb my way in the process.

I brushed it off my sleeve.

"Or maybe someone used it one time to pass a note?" Carly thought out loud.

"Maybe there was more than one time," I said slowly. "If Trudy Tilden wanted out, and the man with the min . . . Bobby buff was looking for something in the walls, and Noah Berkl and Kent Damon were checking out the cooler, there has to be something about the shop, itself. How. Could. I. Be. So. Stupid?"

"Not stupid," Carly said.

Jess added, "Just in the wrong place at the wrong time."

"Like me."

"And me."

Carly grabbed my hand in solidarity. Before this morning, Jess would have been the only one who hadn't been suckered, kidnapped, or otherwise taken advantage of by strangers and acquaintances, but she was full on in the middle of everything now, so she grabbed our hands, too. Being a full-fledged part of the mess was the one good thing to come out of her now regrettable relationship with Bobby.

I plunged ahead. It was time to tell them about what I'd discovered under the flower cooler.

21

"There's something else. Something I found yesterday after I'd closed my shop."

"Your voice sounds kind of funny, Patty. Are you okay?"

"Yea," Jess agreed, "thin, like Mr. Hammerding's voice kind of."

I cleared my throat. The phrase 'full steam ahead' might cause great excitement on a ship full of happy people headed for the Bahamas, but I felt more sea sick than excited.

"I cleaned the cooler Friday."

Jess huffed.

"It's about time. I didn't wanna say anything but . . ."

"Jess, I think there might be more to Patty's statement."

I was sure that Carly would never really ever want to be back with the boys on the plantation, but those few times since she'd escaped that I wondered if maybe she felt a little impatient with us were growing in number. Like just now, for instance. The thing is, even if a friend's question leads you down a different road than you were taking, it does make conversation more interesting. That's why I answered Jess before blurting out what I'd started to say. That and not quite knowing how to explain what I really had to say.

"I know, Jess. It was a little grimier than I thought it was. When you're around something every day you just get used to it and don't notice."

"Like the bathroom sink," Jess pressed her lips together, "and the kitchen cupboards."

Housecleaning can teach you a lot about life. You can start with just one little smudge and if you ignore it long enough, it can turn into a disastrous mess. Of course she was right, but I decided I'd better get to the point before Jess started in on the rest of my apartment.

"Anyway, I had to vacuum up some glass fragments from the cooler . . ."

"Why were there . . ."

I held up a hand. Jess would want every little detail and I might as well start at the starting point and get it done with.

"Noah and Kent were in The Flower Cart Friday."

"Again?"

I nodded to Carly. "They make Melissa nervous and Francis didn't want to go within 20 feet of them, so I walked out there. I actually put them to work."

"Get out." Jess was having none of it.

"Kind of. I handed each of them a flower arrangement from the cooler to put on the counter for me.

"Then Noah said something about knowing I was gone because I'd closed up The Flower Cart and . . . okay, I'm sorry, but I said, 'let's just say I went Vegas with some friends'. I don't know what came over me."

"Wow, Patty."

"Lying to the police?" Jess said at the same time.

"I got a little crazed. You would, too, with hottie FBI guy standing within touching distance."

Jess nodded to Carly in a way that confirmed the truth of Kent's hotness.

"The friend part was true."

"Thanks, Jess. That's what I told myself. That, and I said, 'let's just *say* I went to Vegas blah blah blah' which isn't really saying I went."

"Yea. It's saying 'let's just say' which is something different."

"Oh yea. Absolutely."

"But after they left, I started thinking about their visit. They didn't come back to my office to ask me anything."

"So why . . ."

"They were standing there looking through the glass into the cooler when I walked out and started talking to them."

"I always thought Noah bought his flowers at the gas station."

I nodded.

"He does. But there they were. And so I figured maybe I should try to find what they were looking at or for or whatever. And maybe even what Bobby buff . . ."

I glanced over at Jess. Her face was turning red.

". . . I mean the man with the mints . . ."

Jess was pressing her fingernails into the palms of her hands which were balled into fists.

". . . h-had been looking for when he was there the one time. You know," I continued, grabbing Carly's sketch, "maybe I'm wrong. Maybe it's not him."

I looked down again at the drawing. If the image of the man with the mints was any more accurate, he would've jumped off the page. There wasn't any wiggle room. I laid the picture face down.

"I . . . I don't know why he was there, Jess," I tried to cushion what I'd just said about Bobby, "He probably really did need a greeting card."

Clearly I shouldn't have brought him up again so soon.

"Don't go easy on him, Patty. He doesn't deserve it," came Jess's clipped reply.

Carly reached over and massaged Jess's shoulders a couple of times.

I scratched an eyebrow.

"As I was checking all over the inside of the cooler, I knocked over a vase and broke it.

"So after I vacuumed up the inside and put everything back where it had been, including giving the pink sweetheart rose and baby's breath a new home in a small pottery vase with a picture of a rose on it, I started thinking about how the cooler wasn't as cool as it used to be. I'd noticed it before, but not the kind of noticing that actually leads to thought."

"Aw. I bet it's just the sweetest thing."

The mini-massage had served its purpose.

"Yes, Jess, the new vase is much better than the first one."'

"You should charge more for it," Carly said.

We both looked at her.

"What? It's a practical matter."

I made a mental note. She was right.

"Since the vacuum was already out, I decided to clean the coils. They were pretty dusty."

"The word is dirty, Patty. They probably passed 'dusty' months ago."

"Let me just get to my point, Jess. I was moving right along and pretty proud of myself for taking care of it when the vacuum ran into something. I couldn't tell what it was, though. I used a flashlight to get a better look and—it was a bag. Actually several bags. Well, maybe more than several."

I was getting blank stares. Knowing Jess, she was thinking of a make-up bag and Carly was just plain lost.

"Bags. Like a bag they used to use to carry money in to the bank."

"Like a purse?" Jess asked.

"No. Like a bag, Jess. Like the old khaki green bank bags."

As understanding dawned, they both started looking a little scared.

Carly whispered, "How much?"

Jess slapped my arm.

"Ha. Ha. You really had us going there for a minute, Pattycake."

"I'm serious, you guys. There were bags of money under the cooler."

"And I already asked you how much."

Carly was all business. Jess still looked like she wasn't sure whether to chuckle politely or head for the kitchen again.

"I stopped counting at three."

"Three hundred?" they both said. Their faces had taken on the look of someone who wished she'd found the bags instead of me.

"Thousand. Three hundred thousand."

Carly frowned while Jess scuffed her shoe back and forth on my threadbare carpet.

"Um, which was more: the money you counted or the money you left uncounted?"

"Uncounted. Waaay more uncounted."

"Whyyy did you sit on this until now?" Carly raised her eyebrows and shook her head.

"I tried to tell you! But first it was your visit home and then the car title and everything with it. Then we were all half asleep. And today the thing about Bobby came at us like a bullet."

"A bullet," Jess agreed. Some degree of mad was still in her voice.

After giving them a few minutes to digest my discovery, I continued, "I wasn't sure what to do with it. I mean now I can guess what Kent and Noah and Bobby were looking for, but who put it there, right? Trudy Tilden never struck me as someone who would squirrel that much money away in such a weird manner; and even if she did, she would've taken it with her when she sold the place. To be honest, I can't imagine her making that much in all those years. I know from personal experience a small town flower shop owner will never be a millionaire. And the only other people who are in the shop are me and Francis and sometimes Melissa."

"What about the customers? Is there anyone you can think of who comes in that might stuff something under the cooler when you're distracted?"

We both looked at Carly who immediately realized the impossibility of her question.

"Oh."

"It's okay, Carly. You're just trying to think of everything, which is something we all should be doing. But you know how the store is laid out. I don't think it would be possible for anybody to put something under it without my noticing it. Plus, you need a screwdriver or something to take off the grill at the bottom of the cooler."

"What did you do with the money?" Jess asked.

"At first I was just going to put it back."

"After you vacuumed the bags."

Carly and I both rolled our eyes. There was such a thing as carrying cleanliness too far.

Jess didn't back down.

"If they'd been in there awhile, they were probably pretty dusty, right?"

Oh man. Of course!

I grabbed her by the shoulders. "You're a genius!"

Jess brushed one shoulder like people who are trying to be cool do to show just how cool they are, but Carly scrunched her eyebrows.

"Listen! If the bags had been under there a long time, wouldn't they be dustier than the rest of it? And if the bags had been under there a shorter time, wouldn't they show less dust than the floor?"

Jess and Carly scooted to the edge of their seats.

"They were the same. When I shined the flashlight on everything I noticed it. I just didn't think about it. The same amount of dust was on them as was on the floor and the coils!"

"Which means they'd been sitting there as long as you hadn't vacuumed," Carly said turning it over in her mind.

"Which means they've been there since just before you bought The Flower Cart from Trudy Tilden!" Jess slapped her knee in triumph.

"But what did you do with the money?" Carly persisted.

It was a good thing Carly was there. Who knows what detour we would have taken?

"Oh yea. I was going to leave it, but I didn't want it messing with the cooling system. I moved them to the storage closet, but the lump they made under the old tarp I hid them with was too noticeable."

"Thank heavens," Carly muttered, "closets are the worst place to hide anything."

"There were too many of them to fit in my desk drawers . . . so I ended up putting them back under the cooler. I figured if I laid them more flat than in a bunch, maybe they wouldn't disturb the air circulation so much."

"Look at you: thinking about air circulation," Jess teased.

"I think it's progress, right?"

"Yea, Carly, I think maybe, but you'd better keep keeping a record because I can't keep it all straight."

It was progress, alright, but it was progress like the progress when you're spring cleaning. Before everything is put back in its proper place and beaming at you all clean and shiny-like, things get dirtier than they were before you started and you're standing in the middle of a mess.

22

It was unfortunate that Jess couldn't continue sleeping on my couch, because it was so much easier to try to sort things out when we were together as much as possible. If one of us had an idea or a suspicious dream or anything else in the middle of the night, we could wake up the other ones to get their opinions. It was like one long, extended middle school sleep-over; except we were a long way from middle school, and there was a lot more at stake than nail polish and lunchroom rumors.

Don't get me wrong. I'm not saying they're not important. Carly had started wearing black nail polish around the time we were experiencing the thrill of having the suffix 'teen' in our age. Fortunately, Jess had noticed before it was too late, and we had pulled her back from the abyss by convincing her to wear purple instead. It was a compromise. Jess was already into the shades of pink, orange, and red that fill her world with all things floral. I was still biting my nails, and there wasn't a shade made that I would've worn. While purple wasn't petal pink, it didn't have a picture of a skull and crossbones on the bottle, either.

But the three of us decided Jess would have to go back to living in her apartment so Bobby buff would think everything was just as it always had been. After we got back from Florida, she hadn't had a reason to think about it because they'd only been meeting on the college campus or at odd times in out of the way places he asked her to meet him at. She had been under the impression he'd been working a lot, and until the morning he showed her his house and so much more than he imagined, she'd believed him. After that extremely bad and exhausting day when Jess discovered more about Bobby buff than she had ever wanted to know, she had started telling him she was staying with her elderly aunt to help out after surgery. It avoided his offer to pick her up for their dates since she assured him her aunt needed complete quiet and it would be best if she just met him wherever instead. We weren't really sure about how long a person needed help after surgery, but we figured Bobby buff wouldn't know any more than we did about it.

It was the same reason we had to ditch the idea of getting an apartment together. We couldn't have him stop at a shared apartment to pick Jess up to go to the movies and discover the girl who his cronies had kidnapped and the other one he'd drugged living in the same place as his dear little Dorito. I can't even believe I said that last sentence.

We rehearsed with Jess until she could pull off the lovey-dovey stuff as smoothly as possible. Carly and I took turns pretending to be Bobby buff. We did everything we could think of, from putting an arm around her, to putting a hand on her knee, to brushing a strand of hair away from her face. After all, sacrifices had to be made, and, believe me, we were all making them. Carly even burped loudly to try to make it more realistic, and Jess nodded and said it kind of did.

By the time she walked out the door with her overstuffed duffle bag to return to her apartment, she could look a pretend Bobby buff in the eye without flinching. We just hoped she could do so with the real one.

Two weeks later, I opened the door to the familiar Jess knock which was more like pounding.

"Here," she said, tossing the key to Carly's house in her lap.

"I thought we'd decided you should put it back so Bobby buff wouldn't start wondering anything."

Jess headed for the kitchen and came back with a donut.

"I don't care. Let him wonder all he wants. I'm not giving him back the key to my friend's house. Jerk."

I cleared some papers off of a living room chair so Jess could sit down.

"Is it bad?"

Carly and I knew Jess pretending to be in love when she was recovering from a messy break-up with someone who was unaware they broke up was hard. If she had enough chances to vent, though, it would help, which is why she still spent as much time as possible with us in my apartment and why I asked her the question.

"He was very touchy feely today," Jess groaned. "I nearly slapped him.

"Oh, don't worry," she continued when she saw our faces, "I pulled his hands up to my lips and kissed his fingers instead."

"Nice one. I wouldn't have thought of that."

I really wouldn't have. The only fingers I would ever come close to kissing were made of chicken.

"That's why they call me Jessarino, the Academy Award winner," Jess answered dryly, "So when are you going to visit your house again?" she said, turning to Carly.

Carly shrugged.

"I don't need to go back right away. The smell bothered me anyway, and I can't really clean it without whoever goes there noticing, can I?"

"*You* could," I suggested to Jess.

Jess tilted her head this way and that, thinking it over.

"Eh. Maybe I can ask Bobby to see the house inside and then offer to fumigate it, but I'll say something like 'straighten it' instead."

We nodded and Jess went to get a can of cherry cola to wash down her donut and oh so many other things in her life.

"I wish we could take the money under The Flower Cart cooler and go live in the Bahamas," she said from the kitchen.

Carly added, "I wish you guys could pay off your business and college loans."

"I wish I could buy a new car. I could sell The Flower Cart. At least the cooler would work better for the next owner not having the air circulation clogged up with bags."

I was still grouchy about it. Since I'd told Carly and Jess about the fortune in The Flower Cart, we'd come up with different ways to spend it at least once a day. We'd talked it over, though, and were pretty sure we couldn't spend that money without getting in trouble, ourselves. It would turn more than a few heads to see the three of us all of a sudden rolling in clover instead of slogging through life living on a shoestring. But if I couldn't spend it—and I can't say this forcefully enough—at least it shouldn't reduce how effective my flower cooler was.

"As long as I have to continue my relationship from hell," Jess said through the last bite of her donut, "you need to bump into Noah Berkl and get the information he has about the trouble at The Bagel Cafe."

"It would be very cathartic . . ."

"In English, Patty," Jess interrupted.

". . . satisfying to grill Noah as much and as long as he has grilled me."

Satisfying wasn't really the right word, but it was good enough for Jess.

"Maybe we could go back to The Bagel Cafe and run into him."

"Oh come *on*! I never get to go anywhere."

I leaned over and patted Carly's hand.

"We'll get there. I mean, you could go, but the trunk wouldn't exactly be comfortable and the backseat would be too public.

"Anyway, what are the odds of him being there on the same night at the same time as we are, Jess?"

Meeting someone at a restaurant in a small town actually seemed pretty likely compared to the astronomical odds of finding ourselves in the middle of a crime puzzle and having one of us even contemplate riding in a car trunk just to get some fresh air. The irony struck us all at the same time, and we started laughing so hard Carly had to run to the bathroom and Jess fell on the floor, howling. A laugh like that, one that wears you completely out, was what we needed. That, and some luck.

23

I spent the better part of two hours the next day paging through a warehouse catalogue and tapping out a last minute order on the computer as I went. It was the week before Christmas, and although most of my customers had picked up their evergreen swags and wreaths with red bows a month ago, fresh floral arrangements with sparkly lights were still needed for Christmas Eve services in the churches around town. It would be a week more before sparkly lights amped up to the garish stuff people around here preferred for New Year's Eve. I was double-checking the total when luck walked through the door.

I know. I should've posted these particular orders long before now. I was having a bit of a hard time keeping up with everything. That's why I'd brought my laptop to work and was ordering from it. The Flower Cart didn't have anything that technologically current, and I'd always just gone with the flow and ordered from the wholesaler's order form. But now it wasn't like I could go home after work every night and recharge for the next day. Every hour was a working hour, if not running my business, then unwinding the tangle that started the night at The Bagel Cafe. While I preferred to keep my personal computer and business separate, desperate times called for desperate measures. Trust me, it's a saying. I clicked 'send', poured some coffee in a paper cup, slid a sleeve over it, grabbed my own half-drunk coffee, and walked out of my office.

"How're you doing, Noah?" I asked in my friendliest voice.

Noah stood with his hands in his pockets, looking around. He had to pull one out of his pocket when I handed him the coffee. He seemed strangely quiet.

"Noah? Noah, is something the matter?"

"Oh, you know," he sighed, "the wife has everything bought and wrapped already for Christmas and I don't have anything for her yet."

"A lot of men wait until the 23rd or 24th. You're doing great!" I encouraged him.

"Yea?"

I nodded like I knew everything, "Oh yea."

I took a sip of coffee and he took one, too.

"I can suggest a few things if you want or . . ."

I had a sudden thought.

"Or you can come with me back to my office and take a load off. Drink your coffee. We can figure out some ideas from the comfort of a chair?"

Noah seemed relieved to not have to make an immediate decision and headed back there ahead of me. He must really be in bad shape. I didn't know his wife, but I'd seen her around town. She matched Noah in every way there was to match mediocrity, which is to say they seemed like a great match. I'm no marriage guru, but I *have* observed that in most cases the wife outpaces the husband by at least two to one and maybe ten to one when it comes to holidays and gift-giving. I don't know why that is, but with an exception here or there, it seems pretty standard across the board.

"So Noah," I said after I'd nixed his ideas of sexy lingerie and small kitchen appliances and suggested some new scrapbooking tools, pages, and stickers (his wife was one of those that like that sort of thing) and, of course, a gift basket of all things chocolate mixed in with a red sweetheart rose arrangement—a special that I happened to be running all week.

"How's it going down at the station?"

He gave a sideways nod.

"Shoplifting picks up this time of year, but the snow doesn't give us as many speeding tickets. That's not really my area though."

He looked like he was getting ready to go.

"Can I get you another cup of coffee?" I grabbed the coffee pot and poured him another cup. "How's the case about the Bagel Cafe thing going?"

Noah studied me for a minute.

"Why?"

I gave a half-shrug.

"It's hard for me to forget about, you know, what with being questioned every so often."

My explanation must have made sense to him, because Noah settled back in the chair and nodded.

"I shouldn't talk to you about it."

I held my hands out, palms upward. "Noah. It's me." I said it like we were old friends.

He nodded. "We've run into a bit of a roadblock."

"Yea?"

I sipped my coffee and tried to look only slightly interested.

"There was another crime even bigger than what you witnessed on August 8th, and the lead we thought we had on it disappeared."

"What happened?"

That was an innocent enough question, I thought.

Noah leaned in and whispered, "It was a girl about your age—she was abducted. There was an FBI agent who came here to put her in witness protection when the robbery happened, and somebody scooped her up. There was a big investigation over it. The agent who was lead had to go before Internal Affairs"

I shook my head like I thought it all was a pity. He had no idea how much of one.

"But he was exonerated."

"Ah ha. Is that agent still involved in finding out what happened to . . . the girl?"

"I don't know. FBI—we don't usually work together. Maybe they pulled him off the case as punishment. Maybe not. I don't know much about that stuff."

"But you're working with an agent."

Noah nodded and crossed his legs.

"We started thinking the two events might be related, so they asked him to come down here for awhile. Nice guy. Not like some of them."

I nodded, thinking of Kent's chocolaty eyes.

Noah uncrossed his legs and moved to the edge of the chair again like he was getting ready to leave. I grabbed a candy bar from my desk, tossed it to him, and jumped up to get him some more coffee.

"Here," I said as I poured him the third cup he hadn't asked for as he unwrapped the candy.

"It's nice just chatting for a change, isn't it?"

Things were coming out of my mouth that I would never have dreamed.

Noah sighed.

"Yes, Patty, it is. There isn't enough of that type of thing anymore these days."

"Are you going somewhere for Christmas?"

"No, the wife's family is here, so we go to her sister's on Christmas and then the pack of them come to our house for New Year's Day. I don't mean to sound resentful."

I frowned and shook my head, "You don't sound the least resentful."

Noah let out a grateful breath.

"And look at you! You're getting your Christmas shopping done with time to spare!"

"Yea, I guess I am."

"I suppose your wife got all the decorating done weeks ago."

"Oh yea. She loves that stuff. It looks nice."

"I'm sure it does."

"We got a fake tree this year. Not as much to clean up afterwards." Noah's voice sounded a little sad.

"Fake or live—both are good. Think of the pretty lights and . . . and things. And the downtown! I love the Christmas tree by the courthouse this year. Did they get new lights?"

"Mmm, more, I think. They have some old and some new, I think."

"So, just out of curiosity, what was the lead you had that disappeared?"

Noah looked confused.

"You know, the lead about the bigger crime?"

"Ah. Well, the FBI thought they had a bead on the place the girl was kept at. But when we went in with SWAT, it was as clean as a whistle. No girl, no evidence of there being a girl—just some bachelors who prefer the peace and quiet of living out of town."

"You've got to be kidding!"

I shouldn't have let loose like that, but it was pretty distressing to hear Carly was nearly rescued, even if she had already rescued herself.

Noah frowned.

I cleared my throat. "I guess I was getting into your story more than I thought. Heh heh. Um, when did this happen?"

"Only a few weeks ago. I hate to say this, but that girl is probably dead or long gone."

I nodded, trying not to think of 'the girl' who was probably munching on apple slices on my couch at this very moment. Instead, I had to think of what I could say to prolong a conversation that probably should never be taking place and never would have, but for Noah's Christmas present desperation and subsequent gratitude to me for helping him out of it.

"Kent said he wonders if there's a leak in our department."

"You mean like a bad cop?"

Noah nodded. "Or more than one."

He looked distressed, and ran his hand over his head.

"How many more?" I asked, "Than one?" I added.

Noah stared at the wall behind me and his eye twitched a couple of times.

"You know, Patty, time was when you trusted the badge. I don't know what this world is coming to."

If I was the sort that hugged, I would've hugged him. It must be a sorry state of affairs when you can't even trust your co-workers.

"I can call Linley's downtown and ask Barb Mercer to pull some scrapbooking things together for you. Then all you have to do is pick them up and pay for them.?"

Noah nodded quickly, looking appreciatively at me like he was a cold little planet and I was the sun. It was worth the relatively quick call to keep him from leaving. He was getting more fidgety by the minute.

"Did they give up? On finding the girl?"

"Nooo. They'd never give up, but some things get pushed to the back burner after awhile. They've got bigger fish."

"Oh?"

"I've said too much already."

"I bet it has to do with what the girl was being put into witness protection for, huh?"

Noah raised his eyebrows.

"I should've been a detective!" I laughed nervously while Noah laughed, too. "So why were you and Kent Damon in here the other day?"

"Ha. You remember his name alright. I told him when we left you were just playing with him when you acted like you didn't remember his name."

Noah got up.

"I'll pay for the chocolate and rose arrangement now," he said.

I started to the coffeepot again, but he walked out to the counter, so I had to follow him.

I took his money and rang it up for his receipt.

"Thank you. I'll have Francis deliver it on the 23rd if that's okay. We're closed Christmas Eve and Christmas."

Noah nodded.

"But really. Why were you and Kent here?"

Noah laughed, shook his head, and waved as he walked out the door.

24

"You will never believe this!" I called as I walked into my apartment.

Carly and Jess looked up from their Subway sandwiches. I stopped short.

"You did *not* go to Subway without me."

Carly reached into the bag on the table and held out a toasted sweet onion chicken teriyaki with the works.

"Jess picked them up on her way back from classes."

Jess's mouth was full, so she nodded. I went to the kitchen for a cherry cola.

"Anyone want one?" I called over my shoulder.

"I do."

"Make that two."

It was good to have one normal thing back in place.

"No Bobby buff tonight?"

Jess rolled her eyes.

"Thank heavens. He said he has some work keeping him late. I cooed at him and hung up."

"So what will we never believe?" asked Carly.

Between bites of a sandwich that was clearly what all sandwiches should strive to be, I told them about what Noah said about how the SWAT went out to rescue Carly, but they didn't find anything.

Jess leaned in.

"SWAT? Did he say how many there were?"

"No, Jess, not the number nor their names nor addresses."

I patted Jess's arm.

"Didn't they find anything at all? I had a few clothes there that they'd bought me. Not much, but still."

I shook my head.

"Or the shed? Did they look in the shed? There was a cot out there for me. And a heater and a fan."

"He didn't say anything about the shed. Even if they did look in there, don't you think the guys would've gotten rid of anything you'd used after you got away? Let's say Gunns and Mike didn't even tell the others about you ditching them until they got back. The others would've been told by now. They've had enough time to get mad and then talk it over and figure that they'd better get rid of everything having to do with keeping you there. I mean, why would they keep it? The only thing it would accomplish would be to provide evidence you'd been there."

Carly pounded on the table.

"I want those guys to pay!"

I touched her throbbing hand.

"We all do," I reassured her.

"They won't stop looking for you, Carly," I remarked as Jess licked mayonnaise from her finger.

Jess gave me a look as Carly's shoulders slumped.

"I'm sorry, but it's true. I was right in the first place about Carly not going out in case someone recognized her. They're not going to want to leave someone alive and running around who can identify every single one of them. Now that the police went out there, they're for sure going to want to tie up loose ends, if you know what I mean."

Carly and Jess froze. I mean maybe we'd kind of thought of it before. We knew we didn't want there to be any possibility of them seeing her on the street. We'd thought they probably wouldn't be around this town much, since they lived far enough out that they probably slink into another town's grocery store for pizza and what not. Probably not soap. What we hadn't thought about was them driving around and actively looking for her.

"It's okay, it's okay," I lied, "And there's another thing."

"Patty, we're having a moment here. We're still feeling all kinds of terrified, and you're going on to the next thing like it's nothing!"

Jess reached for the half-eaten sandwich in front of me, took a bite, and put it down. I shoved the rest of it over in front of her.

"I just think we've got to keep moving forward, you know?"

Carly nodded at me to keep going.

"Another thing Noah told me is that they think the Bagel Cafe thing and Carly's abduction are connected."

"Well that makes so much sense," Jess responded. "Carly getting kidnapped to keep her from testifying about something she doesn't know about and you losing your hearing in one ear during a robbery are clearly related." She huffed just to make sure we knew how stupid she thought it was.

"And," I continued before Jess started elaborating.

"Kent told Noah he thinks there could be a dirty cop or even more than one in the department."

"Police or FBI?"

"Huh. Police. I think. I think it was," I repeated, mulling it over in my mind.

"Because he was talking about how maybe Gunns and the gang had been tipped off. But he didn't say their names, of course."

I started clearing Carly's sandwich wrappers from the table, and Carly wiped it off.

"Can we go for a drive?" she asked suddenly.

"*Now*? Guys looking for you? Tying up loose ends? Does that possibility mean anything to you?" Jess said, frowning and taking another bite of my sandwich.

Carly threw the dishcloth in the kitchen sink, then walked around the living room, then sat down again. It took a few seconds.

"I feel like a caged animal in here. Maybe we can drive by my house. It'll make me feel a little more normal, you know?"

The expression on Jess's face went from disapproval to sympathy in less than a minute. She put her hands up like they were stop signs.

"If we're going to go out, we might as well make a night of it.

"C'mon. Fix yourself up. You too, Patty."

"Nuh uh uh. Are you guys listening to yourselves?"

Carly turned puppy dog eyes on me.

"No! No! No! No! What did we just get done talking about? Carly probably has a big red target on her back."

Jess gave me a very effective look of yearning.

"And us by association!"

Carly sat down again and scrunched her legs underneath. The cushion, while not in that great of shape to begin with, had taken on a Carly-shaped dip in the middle. I don't know why I hadn't noticed it before. Maybe it was because I had been caught up more in our collective questions than the longing now coming at me from two quarters of the room.

Carly switched on the TV. There was nothing good on. She switched it off again and started paging through an old magazine she'd already read every word of more than once.

Jess looked accusingly at me, then tilted her head toward Carly.

"Aughhh! Okay, but Jess, fix ourselves up? Really? We wouldn't leave the car; and, again, I don't even think we should leave my apartment. At least not Carly."

Carly jumped up and ran to change out of my sweat pants and into my jeans and one of Jess's sweaters she'd left behind for her.

"I think I need this, Patty. I just need to get out. Clear the cobwebs. Besides, it's dark. No one can see anything in the dark. Hey! We can pretend we're out for a night on the town. Like, you know, drive past the theater and slow down a little. That will be going to a movie."

"Yea," Jess added, "we can slow down by The Bagel Cafe and pretend we went out to eat!"

"That's one slow down for two places since they're across the street from each other," I mumbled. "After that we can slow down by the landfill out of town and pretend we went to the dump."

"I heard that," Carly called from the bathroom.

She came out looking better than I'd seen her look since the night at the Bagel Cafe. Her hair was pulled back, she had on a touch of mascara and lip gloss, and her eyes were sparkling.

Jess started doing a little happy dance.

I sighed. There was no fighting the two of them.

By the time I'd made myself look presentable and gone out to make sure the coast was clear, an hour had passed and just a sliver of moon was high in the sky.

We had more fun than I cared to admit. It was like old times when we'd drive around just for the sake of it. As we were turning on to Carly's street, Carly started pounding on the back of the front seat.

"Let's go in."

Jess and I looked at each other.

"C'mon. Look. See? No lights. No one's here. We don't even need to turn on the lights. We can use the flashlight you always carry in the glove compartment, Patty."

I started shaking my head and Jess's leg started going up and down.

"Pleeease? Look there. We can park a few houses down. No one will even see a car in the driveway."

If anyone else would've asked me to do such a ridiculous thing considering everything, I would've driven right on by. But it was Carly, and after her experiences of the past seventeen months, it was pretty hard to say no to her going into her own house. I wish I would've remembered that sometimes saying no to a friend is the smartest thing to do.

25

We tried to stay out of sight by crouch-walking by hedges and trees until we finally reached the back door. Carly unlocked the door with the key Jess had swiped from Bobby buff's house, and we bumped into each other hurrying to get in. By this time Jess was giggling. Maybe it was because fear was coursing through our veins like a Ferrari, but it was all we could do to keep from outright guffawing until we were all inside.

"Eeesh. I can see what you mean by smell."

Jess grabbed the flashlight from me and shined it around until she had explored every corner of the kitchen.

"I just can't," she said as she grabbed a paper towel and glass cleaner from under the sink and started spritzing every possible surface.

I grabbed her hands.

"You can and you will. Do you want someone knowing we were here?"

"Knowing who was here, Patty? They don't know you. They don't know me."

I huffed.

"Okay, Bobby knows me, but he's not going to think of me in connection to this house. The only one they know is Carly."

"So they know Carly. Do you want them to think Carly was here?"

Jess put the glass cleaner back and took a few swipes over the places she'd spritzed.

"Jessicaaa."

"You said I should clean this up when we talked about it before," Jess reminded me. "Anyway, I can't leave glass cleaner spray on anything. Okay. See? No more paper towel," she answered as she tossed it in the wastebasket.

"Not the wastebasket!" I snapped.

Jess sighed, pulled the entire liner out of the wastebasket and replaced it with a new one. Then she started picking things out of the garbage bag in front of her and putting the non-smell-producing ones back into the new liner.

I slapped my forehead.

"What? Look. I'm sorting through things now. Maybe there's something that will help us know more about these guys and what's going on," she said, shining the flashlight on pieces of paper and mail. "Trust me, if they're anything like Bobby, they won't notice anything about the wastebasket or the smell."

I left her sorting through things with the flashlight and went to look for Carly who had moved unerringly through the house a minute after we'd walked through the door.

"Carly!" I hissed.

I heard floorboards creak overhead and ran up the stairs.

A large duffel bag was open on Carly's bed and she was leisurely going through her closet, selecting things to put in it.

"Oh, hi, Patty," she said like we were at the park on a summer day.

I sat down on the bed.

"Here. Just give them to me. I'll fold them and pack. It will speed things up."

"You really are spooked, aren't you?"

I nodded. I just didn't feel good about this.

I jumped when I heard Jess clomping up the stairs like the Jolly Green Giant.

She dropped the garbage bag and threw herself down next to me on the bed. Holding the flashlight under her chin, she made a disgusted face.

"I should've set it outside the door," she said, pointing to the garbage, "but I thought I shouldn't open the door more than necessary in case it attracted the neighbors' attention. I didn't see much except another insurance receipt and junk mail. I put most of it back, but there's a little that I left under old pizza crusts and something moldy that I didn't want to touch. You can look through the rest when we get back to your apartment."

"Gee thanks, Jess."

"I think that's it," Carly said, closing her closet door.

That wasn't it, though, because she started rummaging in her drawers and throwing some things in my direction. It was good Jess was there to help me fold because Carly was going at it with both hands. Suddenly, she straightened.

"Did you hear that?" she whispered.

We listened as hard as we could. A car engine was running in the driveway. Carly ran to her window and looked down.

"Oh no! Oh no! No no no! Someone's coming in!"

"The key!"

Jess patted her pocket, "I have it."

"Did we lock the door?"

Of course we hadn't.

"Turn off the flashlight, Jess!" I whisper shouted.

We heard the door knob turn, the door open, and three sets of footfalls.

I put my hand firmly on Jess's knee to stop it from jiggling and motioned to the closet door.

Carly shook her head, and pointed under the bed. The three of us dived under it, pulling the duffel bag and the garbage with us. It was a bit crowded.

The thing about bad smells is that they're at least semi-tolerable from a distance. When they're shoved up right next to you, it's another story. Jess started gagging. Carly put her hand over Jess's mouth.

I shushed them.

"Listen," I whispered, pointing to the floor.

Light switches were being flipped on. A faint gleam shone up the stairway, not quite reaching Carly's room.

There was some indistinct conversation we couldn't understand. We could hear their steps: one sounded like heavy work boots, the other two were just normal footfalls, maybe tennis shoes.

Carly wiped some tears from her eyes. She mouthed the words, "It's Gunns and Mike and one of the other guys. It sounds like Gemini."

"Waaat?" Jess mouthed.

"Ge-min-i." Carly waved her hand back and forth like it didn't matter that much.

I put my finger to my lips.

"You got lucky this time, seein's how the key's missin'."

"I'm tellin' you, it wasn't me! The key was with Simpson. Maybe that stacked chick he sees took it."

They laughed loudly.

It was unfortunate that, although we couldn't understand much of the conversation, the last comment rang as clear as a bell. I could feel Jess starting to boil like a lobster in New England.

From the few words we could understand, it sounded like they did some drug dealing out of Carly's house, and were there to meet a buyer. There was some language we didn't want to hear and noises downstairs like they were looking in the cupboards to see if there were any stale munchies. After awhile it sounded like they'd moved to the living room and had settled back munching on something.

"There were some Girl Scout cookies in the freezer. Maybe they're eating them."

"I don't think it matters what they're eating, Carly."

Jess gagged for the fourth time.

Sounds from the T.V. drifted up to us, and Jess pushed the garbage bag away so it was sticking out from under the bed. It was a relief for all of us.

Screams, gun shots, and generally scary music grew louder.

Carly was breathing heavily and Jess's eyes were so wide I could see their whites even by the dim moonlight.

"Do you think they'll come up here?" Jess asked.

Carly and I shrugged as well as we could in our cramped state.

We heard another scream from the T.V. and someone begging for mercy. I felt sick.

Gunns and Gemini bantered back and forth, and though we could understand bits and pieces, most of it was unintelligible.

When we'd scrambled under the bed, we hadn't had time to arrange ourselves comfortably. Carly's head was crammed against the wall. Jess's knee was jabbing into my back, and my arm was pinned under her torso. By now our legs and arms were starting to either fall asleep or cramp. If we moved, though, the floors would creak, so our options were limited to tingling limbs and muscle cramps.

"You think the Feds know what went down at that restaurant?"

There was a loud laugh and more talking, some of it puzzling. Then one of them said something about grabbing "the girl" and the kid with her diving to grab her.

I automatically put my free hand over Jess's mouth just as she whispered "aw" and got my hand wet.

"I kinda wish we hadn't lost her. We could've sold her in Miami like Simpson said to."

Carly gasped.

They stopped talking. Carly was pressing her lips together as though it would make the noise she'd just made non-existent. Jess put her hands over her face like it would stop whatever was going to happen to us if they found us. I started praying to the Lord Jesus like we were best friends.

We could hear someone coming up the stairs. Jess slowly pulled the garbage bag back under the bed which immediately led to more gagging.

Whoever it was stopped in two bedrooms and the bathroom, knocking things over and opening closets. He was nearing Carly's door, when a voice called up the stairs.

"Anything?"

"Na. It must've been the wind or something. I'm just gonna check one more room."

The guy took a few steps closer and stopped. All of a sudden Jess started taking a bunch of short breaths, which you would think she would avoid at all costs considering her aversion to the garbage. Carly and I realized her problem at the same moment and piled on top of her head as much as possible to stifle her.

The door slammed against the wall at the very second of Jess's muffled sneeze. Whoever was checking the upstairs had clearly not taken his mother's efforts to teach him the polite way to open and close doors to heart, and, at the moment, we were extremely grateful he was a slow learner.

He switched on the light, and we could hear hangers moved to the side in the closet. There was a pause. By now I was talking to Jesus like we were both members of an old family who knew each other's secrets and still loved each other anyway. At the moment I was simultaneously thanking him profusely that we hadn't hid in the closet and begging to become invisible.

Jess grabbed my hand and squeezed it so hard I nearly bit her to make her stop. Carly put one hand over her face. We held our breath.

Then we saw them: a pair of tennis shoes standing so close we could've touched them with little effort. They disappeared as he lay down on Carly's bed. It was almost as if whoever it was was just lying there daydreaming as Carly had done the first time she'd gone back to her house; and it made him seem almost normal.

Finally, he got up, switched off the light, and went back downstairs. The three of us let out a collective sigh as quietly as possible.

Something was said by the person who'd searched the upstairs. Then Gunns, Mike, and Gemini must have lost themselves in the story on T.V. because there wasn't much talking.

After awhile Jess whispered, "Maybe Gunns figured out we're here and they're just biding their time until they come up here for the big reveal."

"It wasn't Gunns. I think it was Mike. But no, I don't think so. Those guys never do anything that requires patience."

Around 1:00 in the morning, it sounded like someone came in the back door. A conversation began normally enough, but became louder and more heated with every minute. It was something about money. Someone pounded his fist on the wall and there were two gunshots. We heard a thump, some more shouting, threats, then someone running out of the house with two sets of footfalls right behind.

Before we could stop her, Carly shot out from under the bed and ran down the stairs. By the time we joined her, she was leaning over a dead body. Blood was beginning to spread on the carpet.

"Mike." She patted his chest like it would comfort him.

"Oh this is bad. This is bad," Jess squeaked.

Jess and I looked at Carly and the body on the carpet. He looked like any guy you'd meet on the street. I looked at his feet. He was wearing the tennis shoes we'd seen up close just a couple of hours before. He was the one who had stood so closely to us as we hid under the bed, and he was the one who had lain down on the bed like every other person who just wants to rest and dream and think.

"We've got to get out of here," I muttered.

I ran and got a washcloth to wipe Carley's fingerprints from Mike's shirt, but when I came back she had a funny look on her face, and was examining something. Without a word, she held it out to me.

It took just a glance for me to recognize the handwriting.

"Where did you get this?"

Carly patted Mike's shirt pocket. I held it up for Jess to see.

"How?"

Carly shook her head and shrugged, but Jess was all over it.

"Oh, oh, oh. You said he was a year younger than you?" she asked, looking at Carly.

Carly nodded.

Jess made a continuing motion with her hand. "And had seen you in school?"

"And?" I asked, because I wasn't catching up yet, though a look of understanding had dawned on Carly's face.

"And so he'd seen Carly with her friends . . ."

I was still shaking my head.

"And knew you were her friend . . .

"Oh for pete's sake, Patti. He could figure out your address."

"And he sent you the letters to keep it in front of you. In his own weird way, he was asking for help." Carly spoke so softly we had to lean in to hear her.

Maybe she was right. Maybe Mike was better than anyone ever knew and was locked into the same bad situation as Carly, only on the other side of it.

Carly didn't say anything when I moved her hand and began wiping any part of him she might've touched. Her eyes and nose were red and she started rocking back and forth.

Jess dropped Carly's duffel and the garbage by the door while I looked out a window onto the street. It was empty and quiet, but who knew for how long? The neighbors might think they heard a TV show or a couple of stray firecrackers, but we couldn't count on it. And what if Gunns and Gemini returned?

"Carly, I'm sorry about Mike, but we've got to get out of here."

Carly nodded and joined us at the door. The night air helped soothe us a little.

Despite our worries to the contrary, no one was hiding behind the next corner, and we hightailed it down the street to my car under cover of darkness and relief mixed with fear.

We'd had more excitement than any of us expected while we were fixing ourselves up for a night on the town. One good thing came out of it. Carly said she would never again feel like a caged animal in my apartment because it was the most beautiful, coziest place in the world.

26

The other good thing that was a result of being trapped under Carly's bed and scared out of our wits for three hours was that we learned more about the robbery at the Bagel Cafe. We also heard a name we hadn't heard of before; and for some reason it made us think he was one of the dirty cops Noah had mentioned. And we found out they were using Carly's house as a place to—in her stubborn words—"deliver" drugs.

Carly turned into a mess for at least a week. Whether she really liked Mike or simply felt gratitude was hard to say and she wasn't saying. What she *did* say was that she thought he'd figured out she was under the bed, but didn't tell the guys downstairs. I kind of thought she was slipping into Stockholm Syndrome mode. But what if she was right? Even the possibility of it made Jess and me join her in gratitude, misdirected as it might have been. Plus, there was the letter from Mike's shirt pocket, now resting on top of the other letters, which had, in one night, transformed from threatening into a clumsy effort to be helpful. But Mike wasn't going to hear our thanks since he'd been shot in the process of what we could only conclude was the night's deal gone sour, and he would lie there until the plantation boys dragged him out or someone discovered him. Carly seemed comforted that he was "safe" in her house. There are some things that can't be explained.

I read somewhere one time that eyewitness testimony isn't always dependable because two people can see the same thing and recall it differently. I remember thinking at the time that even if that were true, having more eyewitnesses rather than fewer would paint a clearer picture, what with all those versions: kind of like the story about the blind men describing an elephant differently depending on the part of its body they touched. In this case, I was one of the blind men. I had seen things, but now after long consideration, I had to admit I saw them wrong.

The first wrong thing that I thought I'd seen but hadn't was that what happened wasn't just a robbery. It was first and foremost a distraction. It's a good thing, I guess, that I hadn't known that, because knowing that I'd witnessed something to do with Carly being kidnapped would have driven *me* to distraction. And I had enough of that in my life with the letters every month. And with Jess.

I started piecing the trouble at the Bagel Cafe together again. It started when some chairs were knocked over and three people to my left hit the floor. I thought about those people, and the more I thought about it, the more I was convinced that they were the same ones being questioned at the police station along with me that night. Except for the people who worked at the Bagel Cafe, everyone else had run out before the police arrived.

Next, I heard something going on behind the counter to my left and saw the reflection of a man's face in the window to my right, but he wasn't the same man who grabbed money from the cashier at the end of the counter which was slightly behind me and to my left. Someone by the door noticed I was looking at the reflection of the extra guy. I'd been concerned with one thing: a robbery and who did it. Now I was considering the things that took place in addition to the robbery, itself. I was looking at the background instead of the main picture, and when I did that, there was more to see.

For instance, whose reflection did I see in the window, and who was standing by the door and saw me looking not at the thief, but at the third man? One more question: was the cashier simply very cooperative or was he in on it? I shook that idea from my head. I was pretty sure he was down at the station, too, still shaken from the whole ordeal. I knew him from looks only. His family had moved to town not even a year before. I felt better when I remembered that.

The third thing to reconsider was the lady who screamed and fell forward like she was dead when I heard the gunshot. From the snatches of conversation we'd heard the night Mike was shot, I now knew she was no lady. She was the girlfriend of someone by the name of Dickie, and Carly had told us that Dickie was part of the group that held her captive. If he was part of that group, he likely shared their habits of dirty speech and hygiene. The person sitting a few tables away might have been insecure. She might have been gullible. She might have been as rebellious as he was. But someone who would date a guy who used foul language and committed a crime that she knew about was no lady.

The fourth thing I got wrong was that there was no gunshot. It was a flash bang grenade tossed by my left ear. The last time Noah had questioned me (the first time I'd met Kent Damon, FBI), I'd been told I was the only one who said there was a gunshot. I was the only one who thought someone was shot. I could believe that some others saw the grenade being tossed, and figured out the sound came from it, but how could I have been the only one who didn't figure it out? I was pretty sure I'd turned again to look at the reflection in the window. Did the police think that since it was so close to me that I was the one who dropped it there and that I claimed there was a gunshot in order to mislead them? Or since my statement was different than the others' from that night, did they think I was lying?

And who, anyway, had I given my statement to that first night? I hadn't seen him afterward, even when I was at the police station the additional times I was questioned. But that first policeman had been the one who had written down what

I said. What if he was a dirty cop and wrote down more than I'd said? Or wrote down something different entirely?

The more I thought about it, the more I kept thinking about the reflection in the window. I was looking at that reflection just before the flash bang.

"Are you going to see who's there, Patty?"

The sound of Francis' voice pulled me out of August 8th and back to the present. Someone had come in and was walking around the room looking at things. I could tell by the sound of her kitten heels on the floor that it was Mrs. Baxtrom.

She walked over to the flower cooler and peered inside.

"Mmm. Some nice roses today. They're perfect for the flower show planning committee meeting this evening. I'm so glad the cold weather will be behind us soon."

She placed her order and then looked at me. I sighed.

"Yes, Ma'am. Two dozen roses: six red, six white, six pink, six yellow."

Mrs. Baxtrom nodded her head slightly and cocked it to one side waiting for me to finish. I repeated the delivery address back to her. Now we could all rest easier being sure I could read the address she'd given to me a moment before. Otherwise, you know, I might send it to the Queen of England or something, and she clearly doesn't need any more flowers what with the garden party she has every spring.

I mentally slapped myself. Mrs. Baxtrom was a sweet little old lady. She deserved more from me than unspoken sarcasm.

"So you have the flower show meeting tonight?"

"The flower show planning committee meeting, yes."

"I suppose it's nice to get together with those folks."

"Mmm?"

"You all like the same thing. Things like that."

"Hm. Yes. Most of the members have been on the committee for years."

"So I heard the weather forecaster say we might reach 60 next week."

"I always appreciate temperate weather."

I nodded.

"Well then you probably really like being at your vacation home in Key Biscayne. The temperature is so much more . . . more . . . temperate down there."

"Why, Patty! How in the world did you remember where my vacation home was?"

"Oh—you know—I guess it just stuck with me."

I'm pretty sure Mrs. Baxtrom would've never believed I'd traveled more than fifty miles in any direction from the town we both called home, much less Florida. Nevertheless, there was no reason to clutter our boring conversation with that little tidbit.

Business started picking up then, and she left while I helped some other customers. Thanks to my vacuuming the coils and smoothing out the money bags underneath it, the flower cooler was working slightly more efficiently and the flowers were already staying a little fresher longer. Even Francis noticed.

"Patty, you mus' be ordering from a different wholesaler. These flowers look real fresh, you know?"

I nodded.

"It must be an extra good batch this time," I mumbled.

Francis whistled while he carried the day's deliveries to the truck.

"Francis?" I asked as he picked up the last arrangement, "you've worked here a long time, haven't you?"

"Long enough, Patty."

"Who delivered the flowers before you did?"

Francis chuckled. "Mr. Baxtrom, he was the delivery guy."

"Mr. Baxtrom! Are you sure?"

Francis nodded.

"Oh yes. His wife, she come to see him sometimes Ms. Tilden tol' me. She never order then. Only after he died."

"Mrs. Baxtrom's Mr. Baxtrom?"

Francis began laughing.

"Yes, Patty. You think I don' know who's before me?"

"So. Huh. So when did he die? It had to be soon after Trudy Tilden changed her flower cart into a store, because I never met him."

"Patty, what's wrong with you? You met him, probably a few times before he cross over."

I shook my head. I really couldn't remember.

"Yes, yes. You worked here in high school."

"You were always the delivery guy, Francis."

Francis nodded.

"Yes. But did you ever come here with friends like the young girls do to look at ribbon? Or flowers for a dance?"

I nodded.

"I'm sure you saw him one or two or three times before he die. He live in dis town long time."

I kept shaking my head.

"He have little bald spot here and here," Francis pointed to the front and back of his head.

I squinted my eyes.

"He have gray mustache. He little taller than me."

I slowly nodded.

"Yea! See? I met him at grocery store I work at before I work here. He was buying steaks. If you ask me," Francis confided, "he and his wife, they very much alike. Arrogant, you know?"

My head was spinning. I'd always kind of assumed Mrs. Baxtrom's dead husband was some kind of CEO who had made loads of money and had stocks coming out of his ears. How else could his estate afford to send her a fresh bouquet every week?

"I just don't understand it. Mrs. Baxtrom's property is huge by this town's standards. Plus she has a vacation home in Key Biscayne. What did he do before delivering flowers?"

Francis shrugged.

"He's been dead long time now. Let him rest. You want something else, Patty? I should get going on these."

I waved my hand.

"Of course. Go ahead. See you tomorrow."

Francis waved as he walked out to the delivery truck, and I sank down in my office chair staring into space.

27

Jess peered over Carly's arm as they studied the list I'd given them. I'd written out the things that happened at the Bagel Cafe the night of August 8th in sequence.

"So what do you guys think?"

Carly sat back and handed the paper to Jess so she could get a closer look at it.

"It's like they said the night we were scrunched under the bed at my house. They robbed the cafe to provide enough of a distraction for them to grab me.

"As far as who was there, I know that Gunns drove the car and Mike grabbed me, so they weren't at the cafe. From what Gemini said, he was there. I don't know about Dickie, but his girlfriend was, according to what Gemini said when we were at my house."

"What?"

"She was the one who pretended to be shot. Haha. What a jokster," I said. I was not amused.

"Maybe they hired people to be there," Jess suggested, "You know, like 'We'll pay you fifty bucks if you have supper at the Bagel Cafe on August 8th and scram afterward.'"

"I suppose you could find people here or there to do something like that as long as they didn't care what the person paying them was going to do and they'd still look innocent."

"Maybe they got free drugs instead of fifty dollars," Carly suggested.

"From the drug 'delivery business'," Jess smirked.

Carly sighed.

"So Dickie's girlfriend was there. The others were paid—however they were paid—customers to fill up the place and take off the minute after it happened. More unfamiliar faces would make it harder for real witnesses to sort things out. The cashier was a guy from school. They're new in town. The cook and waitress. And a couple three people to the left of where we sat. Then there was me."

"And me," Jess raised her hand.

"I am so glad you were in the bathroom for all of it."

Jess nodded as her leg started jiggling up and down.

"The other ones were the guy who got the money, the one whose reflection I saw in the window, and the guy at the door."

"The guy at the door, the guy at the door," Carly muttered. "I wonder if he was the lookout?"

"That makes sense. He just stood there. I wonder if he was there when Alden's cousin came in and bought that cup of coffee?"

Carly scrunched her eyebrows in a v, but Jess waved her hand dismissively.

"He just came in for a coffee," she explained. "He probably just wanted something to sip on while waiting for you and Alden to come out of the theater."

"Because if he was there when Alden's cousin . . ."

"Sam," Carly interjected.

". . . Sam got coffee, Sam could ID him if he remembered him."

"I'm sure Sam went over every little thing after it happened," Carly suggested.

"Aw. You're still sticking up for Alden and his family," Jess crooned.

Carly's face turned pink.

"What does Gemini look like, Carly? Maybe I can figure out where he was in the cafe if I see a picture."

Carly drew a quick sketch in her notebook and handed it to me.

"That's him! That's the guy at the door!"

"Okay, okay, okay. So we know Dickie's girlfriend was the one you thought got shot and Gemini was the lookout. The one we don't know the identity of is the one who took the money. Maybe Dickie? Maybe not?"

Carly and Jess shrugged.

I stood up and stretched. Shoving my hands in the pockets of my jeans, I walked over to the window. I wasn't sure if I should tell Lisa and Carly what I had been thinking since I'd had the conversation with Francis. The waters weren't crystal clear to begin with, and I didn't want to muddy them further.

I didn't realize I'd sighed out loud until Jess said, "Out with it, Patty."

The good and the bad thing about having friends that go way back is that they know you well enough to know when something's bugging you. I came back over and sat down.

"I think the reason I didn't know the thing I thought was a gunshot was really a flash bang—other than Dickie's girlfriend going all drama queen—is that I was looking at the third guy's reflection in the window, the guy who might have been a second lookout. It seemed like he was just standing there, though, kind of observing, like he was making sure things went okay."

"So?" Jess called from the kitchen where she was rummaging around my refrigerator for some mint and whipped cream for her coffee.

"So I haven't been able to figure out why I was looking at that reflection. Why didn't I just turn the minute I glanced at it and look at the real thing?"

Carly shook her head. "That would be what most people would do."

"Right. It would be normal to look over your shoulder at the real deal. Unless there was something about the reflection that bothered you; something that stopped you from turning just then because you were trying to figure something out."

"And?" Jess said as she walked back into the living room, slurping her coffee a la mint.

"It wasn't until today that I remembered why I looked at the reflection so long. I was wondering if I was seeing a ghost."

Jess choked on her coffee and Carly grabbed the flowery pillow Jess had given me as an apartment warming present and squeezed against her chest.

"You know how we are about horror films, Patty!" Jess yelled, swiping her fingers over a few drips of coffee on the front of her shirt.

"We don't even make it to the twenty minute mark. And heaven knows we've tried," Carly mumbled, her face pressed into the pillow she still held to her chest. "Not once has any of us seen an entire scary movie."

"Not once!" Jess added, spilling more coffee on the same spot.

"Explain yourself this instant, Patty, or I swear I'm leaving," Jess threatened, dabbing at the coffee stain on her shirt with a Kleenex.

"Okay, okay. You don't need to get huffy."

Jess shook her head at me like it was off its hinges. "A *ghost*? We are up to our eyeballs in sorting out bad guys from good guys. I have to go out there every day, *every day*, and pretend I'm still in love with someone I don't even want to think about, Carly's essentially exchanged one prison for another, and you're talking about ghosts?"

"It's not the same. Your apartment is way different than the plantation. But I admit the thought of ghosts . . ." Carly audibly shivered.

"Hold on. I didn't say I saw a ghost. I said I was *wondering* if I was seeing a ghost."

Jess went to the kitchen and brought back a box of Twinkies, two of which she'd unwrapped on her way back to the living room.

"Go on," she motioned at me like a school teacher with one of the Twinkies.

"Was it shimmery?" Carly interrupted.

"Mmm, no. No shimmer."

"Could you see through it?" Jess asked. Her voice quavered.

"You know how reflections are. I don't know, but that isn't why I was thinking about ghosts. I was thinking about ghosts because the reflection I saw was of someone who was dead."

Jess jumped from the chair onto the couch and huddled with Carly. Carly huddled back.

"Oh good grief. It's not what you're thinking. I thought I saw Mr. Baxtrom. He'd died before that, though, so I was wondering if I was seeing his ghost. I didn't really even think about it until a conversation with Francis this afternoon. He described Mr. Baxtrom to me and then I remembered."

Carly unwrapped Jess's fingers from her arm one by one.

"So the guy who helped rob The Bagel Cafe looked like Mr. Baxtrom," Carly said as calmly as she could.

We all sat there trying to slow our breathing for a few minutes.

When we were sufficiently calm, I said, "Unless it *was* Mr. Baxtrom."

"Oh for pete's sake, Patty. Stop!" Jess's hand shook as she took another sip of her coffee.

"Not like that. What I mean is, maybe he didn't die like everyone thought he did. Maybe he's still alive."

"Well that explains Mrs. Baxtrom getting flowers from her dead husband every week," Jess said.

"The sarcasm dripping from your voice is puddling on the floor."

"His death was on the local news."

Carly and I both looked at Jess in disbelief.

"What? I listen to the news sometimes. Even when we were younger. Anyway, I remember seeing his picture on the TV and a caption underneath."

"Do you remember anything about what it said? Like what he did for a living?"

Jess shook her head.

"Why would it matter?" Carly spoke up.

"Today at The Flower Cart, I was talking with Francis about how long he's been delivering flowers there and he said Mr. Baxtrom used to be the delivery guy before him."

"No. Way." Jess and Carly said in stereo.

"That doesn't make sense. Mrs. Baxtrom has one of the nicest houses in town. It's not a house you could buy with flower delivery mon. . ."

Carly's voice drifted away.

I continued, "I don't think so, either. I always assumed he was a CEO of some big company or something."

"Yea. Or that he was old money and had a lot of stocks and bank accounts and IRAs and . . ."

"Okay, Jess, we get the idea." I needed to stop her recounting all of the financial terms she could think of before she drifted into things like hotels on Park Place and Boardwalk.

"I wonder how Trudy Tilden got her store in the first place?" Carly got up and started walking back and forth between the door and the windows.

"Making a jump here," Jess said, confused.

I hadn't ever really thought about it, and I bet most other people hadn't either, because Trudy Tilden was one of those people that other people just didn't think about. She had always been the slightly eccentric lady pushing a flower cart around town selling flowers until the day she moved into the building it was in now and became a semi-respectable businesswoman. Carly had a point. It would be pretty hard to finance a loan from the income of a simple flower cart. Then again, I'd been a college student with an incomplete degree and I'd done the same thing.

I started pacing back and forth in the living room. I had signed the papers that made The Flower Cart mine, but I hadn't read all the fine print because the man at the bank seemed impatient for me to just sign on the line. I knew banks didn't just loan money willy nilly. They needed some kind of proof that the person they loaned it to would pay it back. Did Trudy Tilden vouch for me? Someone must have. If so, who vouched for Trudy Tilden?

"Who vouched for Trudy Tilden?" I asked out loud, as Carly and I bumped into each other.

Jess cleared her throat.

"Again. Making a jump from Mr. Baxtrom's job to Trudy Tilden buying The . . . oh."

"Do you think he did it?" I asked, "Do you think Mr. Baxtrom was Trudy Tilden's co-signor?"

"Or," Carly spoke slowly, "maybe he provided the money up front for her to start the business in the storefront."

Jess and I were shaking our heads. It made no sense. Considering the past year and a half, something making no sense was familiar territory.

"Maaaybe," Carly continued, "he had a lot of money just like everyone always thought, and he used some of it to help Trudy Tilden get The Flower Cart,

"Why would Baxtrom finance or help finance a little flower shop?"

It was a simple question. Carly and I stopped in our tracks and looked at each other, then at Jess.

I ran my hand over my head. A rich guy filling the role of flower delivery guy still wasn't computing.

Carly threw up her hands.

"It has to go back to the drug deliveries. That's what all the trouble is about. Obviously."

Since her experience on the plantation, drugs were the reason for everything Carly saw. Maybe she was right, but it didn't seem that obvious to me.

"We don't know how The Flower Cart is involved. Maybe this is it. Maybe Baxtrom used it as a cover for drug deliveries."

"Whoa."

I agreed with Jess.

"Yea, whoa. Because Mrs. Baxtrom might be annoying and all, but she's no leader of a drug ring."

"I meant Mr. Baxtrom, not Mrs.," Carly corrected me.

"Even so. Mrs. Baxtrom married to a criminal?" I persisted. "Nah. He's been dead and gone and whatever you heard at The Flower Cart was heard after he died."

Carly raised a finger. "Unless. Unless your suspicions are right, and he isn't really dead."

I rolled my eyes. No wonder we didn't last long at the horror movies. We had more creepy ideas in our collective imaginations than all of Hollywood put together. We ended up throwing one idea on top of the next until 1:00 in the morning.

It's funny how you end up doing things in life that you would never in a million years believe you would do, but after the night's discussion we all agreed. I would have to make the next delivery of Mrs. Baxtrom's dead husband's flowers myself.

28

I'd let Melissa go for the day and was having a mini showdown with Francis.

"Patty, dis not the way it work," he shook his head.

"Now Francis, I'm the owner. I can make a delivery if I want to."

Francis's eyes were getting big, and he vigorously shook his head back and forth as though doing so would change my mind.

"No, Patty. Mrs. Baxtrom, she get bang boom mad at me if she find out you go."

"It's not her flower shop now, is it?" I said as I picked up the delivery for Mrs. Baxtrom from her dead husband and brought it behind the counter with me where he couldn't reach it.

"You should be grateful. You'll get done sooner!"

Francis muttered all kinds of words I couldn't understand all the way out the door and probably kept muttering them all the way to his truck.

* *

My beat up car chugged down the long drive of Mrs. Baxtrom's estate. The only thing I knew about it was what I'd heard from small town gossip and what I could glimpse from the road nearby in the rare event I drove past it. The drive was lined with black walnut trees that were just budding as they peeked into spring. There were bushes to my right with what I guessed was a profusion of butterflies. I wasn't certain, though, because I wasn't going slowly enough to tell. It could've been a mini whirlpool of dust that my beat-up Nissan was kicking up. Some people take their time when they're nervous. Me, I tend to speed up just to get things over with. So, yes, it could've been dust, but it seemed kind of colorful, and dust tends toward the brown family, so butterflies were a distinct possibility. We'll never know because I had so many other things racing through my mind that figuring it out was way down on the list.

The gravel lane had to be half a mile at least, maybe longer. I pulled onto the blacktopped drive past the sign that said, *Deliveries in the Back*, parked in front of the two story house that stretched farther in each direction than I'd ever seen except maybe a magazine, and rang the doorbell.

I don't know what I was expecting, but I jumped a little when Mrs. Baxtrom opened the door.

"Patty?" Her contralto seemed lower than usual.

I'm amazing, I know. I was in the choir because in a town such as mine, you can be in anything you please as long as you behave yourself. It was there that I learned that contralto is the lowest female choir part. Except in this case, a few boys were assigned to sing it, since none of the girls' voices were that low and the assigned boys' voices were barely there, themselves.

"Hi, Mrs. Baxtrom!" I said cheerfully to her unsmiling face.

"What are you doing here?"

She glanced at the flowers I was holding.

"Where is Francis?"

"Oh, I told him I'd bring these out to you today. They're beautiful, aren't they?" I said as I edged over the threshold.

Mrs. Baxtrom moved to let me in even though I was pretty sure she would've blocked me had she not wanted any part of me touching her. I looked for the closest solid surface and placed the flowers on a long table against a wall by a wide staircase. The table held three candles, an urn, and a small dish, but there was still plenty of room for the flowers. I set them down carefully, turning them to the angle they would show best. I could feel Mrs. Baxtrom's eyes follow me.

"This is very improper, Patty."

I was going to reply that as owner of The Flower Cart it was only proper for me to deliver flowers, myself, to one of my best customers. I was going to say I appreciated her business even though it was technically her dead husband's business. I was going to compliment her on her monstrous home and say what nice weather we were having, but opening my mouth to say those things prevented me from saying any of them.

I don't know if it was a gnat or invisible pollen or what, but whatever it was, I started choking on it, and all of a sudden getting air was the only thing on my mind. Mrs. Baxtrom quickly led me into a living room and I fell into a very comfortable, soft, cushy chair with a green, large palm leaf pattern over yellow. Jess would have approved.

While Mrs. Baxtrom went to get me a glass of water, I looked around. Most of the furniture besides the club chair I was sitting in and its identical match was soft, pale yellow leather. There was a fireplace on one wall. Its mantel held a crystal pitcher and three small crystal cups. I could tell they were just for show. No one would ever drink from something that extravagant. A large painting of a boring parlor scene hung above it. The carpet was some kind of pale green with an indistinct design running every which way over it. The room was very Mrs. Baxtromish.

Suddenly out of the corner of my eye, I saw something move and whipped my head in its direction. If Carly was right and Mr. Baxtrom was alive, it wouldn't do to miss seeing him in the flesh for certain. What I saw was much, much worse.

Carly and Jess were tiptoeing through Mrs. Baxtrom's front door. I nearly fell out of the chair as I frantically waved them out again. Jess waved at me and pressed her lips tightly together to prevent what I could only guess was nervous laughter trying to escape, and they quietly climbed the stairs.

They were just about to the top when Mrs. Baxtrom returned with a bottle of water. I started coughing again, this time out of duty, so they could make it the rest of the way up without attracting her attention. They, at least, did that. I coughed louder as I saw Jess trip on the top step.

"Goodness, Patty!"

Mrs. Baxtrom was all conversation today.

I gulped down some of the water and sat back.

"Do you mind if I sit here and catch my breath a minute?"

I really did have to catch my breath after seeing what I'd just seen sneak up the stairs. My mission to find out if, in the words of Mark Twain, Mr. Baxtrom's demise was greatly exaggerated had just expanded, thanks to my friends who weren't supposed to be there.

Mrs. Baxtrom looked perturbed, but nodded and sat in the chair opposite mine.

"Your husband sure must have loved you to send you flowers even after he died."

Mrs. Baxtrom looked slightly entertained.

"Yes, my Robert, quite a romantic." She blinked kind of fast. "He had it put in his will, you know."

I leaned forward a little.

"When did he die, again?"

"It always seems like just yesterday to me."

"But to the rest of us what would it seem?"

My question apparently amused Mrs. Baxtrom because she just chuckled in her croaky way.

I decided to come at it from another direction.

"Do you ever get tired of it?"

Mrs. Baxtrom frowned.

"I mean, at first it must have just tugged on your heartstrings," I hurried on, "but after so many years, do you ever think it's time to move on? Let the flower thing dwindle?"

I attempted a smile to counter Mrs. Baxtrom's frown. She squinted her eyes.

"Why, Patty! You're worried about me."

I was so far from worrying about Mrs. Baxtrom that you'd need a roadmap to get there, but I went with it and nodded.

"No need, dear."

Her voice had regained its usual condescending note, which was slightly higher than the menacing clef she'd used earlier.

She looked like she was about to usher me out, so I said, "You have a very nice home out here. Your husband must have been quite successful!"

Mrs. Baxtrom tilted her head and gave me another frowny squint.

"He always provided very well for me."

"And for himself. I mean when he was alive."

"Yes."

"I can't remember what he did for a living . . ."

I thought Mrs. Baxtrom would finish my thought and I would get an answer to my question about his being a flower delivery truck driver, but instead she said, "Oh he dabbled in a number of things."

Mrs. Baxtrom scooted to the edge of her chair, so I hurried on.

"What did he die from again? I don't remember."

Mrs. Baxtrom looked offended.

I glanced toward the stairs. There was no evidence of my two friends.

"How is the flower committee?"

"The flower show planning committee?"

"Yea. The flower show planning committee."

"Things are coming along nicely."

"Did everyone like the roses from last time?"

"Mm hm."

I was running out of conversation. It wasn't a surprise. After all, this was Mrs. Baxtrom we're talking about, and aside from when I'm with Jess and Carly, I'm not known for my Chatty Cathy ways like some people are. The two of us chatting up a storm would be on par with monks letting it all hang out during Mass. It just wasn't going to happen.

"Sooo . . . nice weather we're having."

Yep. I'd hit the end of conversational possibilities.

Mrs. Baxtrom motioned toward the door, and there wasn't much I could do but get up to leave. If I could have thought of something else, I would have said or done it, but anxiety over my two slightly insane friends upstairs had finally succeeded in driving every worthwhile thought from my head. I stepped out of the house wondering what they were doing and how in the world they would get out before someone discovered them. Mrs. Baxtrom shut the door with more firmness than I thought necessary. She was probably fumigating the chair I'd been sitting in even now.

I got in my car and peered as hard as I could at the upstairs windows of the house, but saw nothing. I couldn't sit there long without attracting attention. Who knew but that Mrs. Baxtrom would peek out the window to make certain I'd left? So I circled around, followed the sign for deliveries I'd earlier ignored, and turned off the engine. A car and a couple of pick-up trucks were parked in the back, too. I hoped my car would blend in.

I could see why this was where deliveries were made. There was not just a back door, but a wider entry on one side and a pole barn nearby. There were some good sized boxes sitting by the wide entry. I couldn't see in any windows other than two grimy basement windows on the stone foundation, and the house was as quiet as a cemetery on a cold night. I wished something—anything—would happen that would tell me what to do to help Carly and Jess get out of Mrs. Baxtrom's house. I craned my neck to look around, but didn't see a soul. So I hopped out of my car, shut the door with a quiet click, and walked over to the boxes. I glanced down at one of them. What? I bent down to look closer, then kneeled in the dirt to make sure I was reading it correctly.

As I began to pick up a box, something caught the corner of my eye at one of the basement windows. A hand? No. Maybe. What in the world? I walked over and squatted to peer through the grime, and what I saw brought a lump to my throat. Six little children plus a couple of teenagers were down there. One of the teenagers was hoisting a child to the window. It was his hand I had seen. Most of them were just sitting on boxes or the floor, and staring at nothing. They looked a bit spacey, and I wondered if they had been drugged. But the two by the window were making signs to me. Although my friends and I mostly focused on—I might as well say it—the drug running and dealing—I instantly thought of the worst part of what Carly had told us. The other aspect of the business was child trafficking. Hearing about it was bad enough. We'd had some really crummy times of just listening as Carly told us every little thing that she'd seen and experienced those first weeks. Jess and I had both ended up kneeling into the toilet on at least one occasion due to what Carly told us. It had the opposite effect on Carly. It seemed like a relief for her to transfer some of the invisible load she carried on her back to ours. No wonder she gave Mike a pass, since his persuasion with the others had spared her more of it. But hearing about it and seeing it are two different things. The lump in my throat extended to my chest and felt like it would explode.

I frantically pushed at the window, but it wouldn't budge. Of course not. Maybe if I ran something sharp around the edge? I ran to my car and rummaged through the glove compartment. Nothing. I poured the contents of my purse onto the seat. The best I came up with was a pen and fingernail file. I ran them along the edges, but they didn't even damage the paint. So I jabbed at the window edge until they both broke.

I glanced around. It wouldn't do for me to get caught and thrown in with them. I signaled to them that I would try to figure something out. They were clearly trapped. I wished Jess and Carly good luck under my breath, wrestled the box with the attached printout on top of it into my car, and drove back to my apartment.

After sitting for nearly an hour in complete horror and running through every possible way to get those poor kids out of there, I'd calmed down enough to start worrying about where my friends were. Sometimes when horror and worry meet together in one grand clash, a person does something that is so far from dealing with the situation it's like snow in July. Yep. I completely zoned out. Don't judge. People do it all the time. Just look at how Congress handles national troubles.

I put a pan of soup on the stove and some refrigerator biscuits in the oven. The picture of that little hand on the basement window popped into my head and my defense mechanism batted it right out again while I wondered who thought of inventing something that would make it seem like you knew how to cook when all you really did was unwrap. Whoever it was, was a good ol' soul.

Jess and Carly came through the door, breathless and laughing. What I'd seen came back to me again in an instant, and I felt like crying.

Instead I scolded, "What are you guys trying to do? Get yourselves arrested for breaking and entering?"

"We didn't break, we just entered," Jess reasoned

"Besides, we had to see if Mr. Baxtrom in the flesh still lives there."

"Ooo. That sounds kind of ghoulish, Carly," Jess said as she flopped down into a chair.

Carly laughed.

"Some of his clothes were in the closet, but Jess said sometimes people keep a few things like that after a loved one dies. I thought I was the only one."

Jess added, "There were a few other things around—a man's ring. It had to be his, I think. Don't you think? I mean Mrs. Baxtrom wouldn't have an affair, would she?"

"Jess," Carly replied, "How can a widow have an affair?"

"Oh. Right."

"I can't imagine Mrs. Baxtrom having feelings for anybody," I added as the lump in my throat grew.

"Ew. Can you think of her holding hands?" Carly asked.

Her face twisted with the thought.

"Or kissing?" Jess made a grossed out sound. I was pretty sure she was only pretending to throw up.

"But," Carly added, "we were able to look around, something you didn't do, Patty."

If she only knew. But, to be fair, I don't know what we'd thought I would accomplish going there on my own. It was probably a good thing they followed me even though I still got cold feet thinking about it.

"And how in the world can you live with yourself, leaving us up there like that?" Jess asked in an accusing voice.

I threw up my hands.

The timer went off, and Jess went to see what was in the oven. I wouldn't need to dish up a thing.

"So?" I asked after she'd brought soup and biscuits in for all of us. "How did you get out without being found out?"

"We climbed out a window onto the roof . . ."

"You what?!"

" . . . then made our way down another slanty kind of roof, then climbed down an iron trellis at the back."

Jess held up her arms.

"I got scratched. The rosebud thorns on the trellis fought back."

"It's okay, though, Patty. I don't know how you could've helped us anyway," Carly reassured me.

Oh yes. I was the unhelpful one who didn't help when someone was in trouble, so it was understandable. It wasn't as reassuring as she thought it was. Jess, however, wasn't about to let me off, and the minute she didn't, I felt better.

"But you took off," Jess persisted.

I gave her a look that stopped the oncoming tirade and got up. I walked to the door and motioned them over to the box I'd set down next to the entry.

"I found this at the back of Mrs. Baxtrom's house where deliveries are made. Look at it," I tilted the box so they could read the list taped to its top.

"Wait. Isn't that . . ." Carly's voice drifted off as she looked up at me.

I nodded.

"What?"

"It looks like the list you gave me that night we went back to the Bagel Cafe to figure things out, Jess. See?" I pointed to the names and phone numbers, abbreviations, addresses and small map.

"The map Carly brought with her that night of the greasy, smoky party?"

Jess's descriptions weren't always perfect, but we knew what she meant.

"Yea. The party Gunns took me to," Carly confirmed. "Are they the same?"

"I dunno." I pulled the list from my pocket and laid it flat so we could compare the two.

You'd think I would have done it the minute I'd gotten home, but I hadn't even thought of it. It's really something how being horrified, feeling helpless, worrying about your friends, and not doing anything about it can prevent you from thinking clearly.

We studied the lists. There were some names, addresses, and phone numbers that were the same, and some that were different. The abbreviations were similar. The map was identical.

"There's something else."

I walked back to the couch and sat down in case I started hyperventilating at the thought of what I was about to tell them.

Carly and Jess looked at each other like maybe I was going over the edge and they didn't know how to handle it. I motioned for them to sit on either side of me.

"My conversation with Mrs. Baxtrom ended up being rather short."

Jess made an amused noise in the back of her throat.

"I know, Jess. But anyway, she nearly pushed me out of her house when it ended, and, believe me, I tried to think of a way to stay there with you guys upstairs and everything, but . . ."

Carly patted my knee. "It's okay."

"So I drove around to the back. I thought maybe I could see you or something, or at least wait for you back there."

"We parked on the road and walked," Carly explained.

"Oh!" Jess exclaimed, "And that's where you found the box!"

I nodded. "But I also found something else."

My ears started buzzing, and I put my head between my knees for a minute. When I straightened to a sitting position, Carly and Jess were mouthing words to each other.

"There were kids," I whispered.

"What?"

"Kids," Carly whispered for me.

"Where?" Jess was all business at full volume.

"Basement. Mrs. Baxtrom's basement," I started crying. "I tried to get the window loose. My pen and fingernail file broke."

"Oh this is bad. This is bad." Jess was being as helpful as possible.

I turned to Carly. "Do you think they're sold out of Mrs. Baxtrom's basement?"

"Or rented," Carly nodded. "Or beat up. Or used for parties."

"This is bad. This is bad."

"And us with no one to trust," I murmured.

I felt like the last key on the key ring had just been discovered to not fit. We talked about going back, but couldn't figure out a way to break in and get the kids out of there that wouldn't involve murder of either us or Mrs. Baxtrom. Our ideas quickly dwindled to silence.

Finally Carly asked, "Maybe we can tell Noah?"

"This is bad. This is bad."

I put my head in my hands. I couldn't stand it.

We knew Carly had overheard or seen something that would implicate whatever the plantation or other business did. We wondered if her parents had been killed to leave her more easily open to harm. We had a partial idea of who'd cause the commotion at the Bagel Cafe as a distraction for Gunns and Mike to take Carly out from under the nose of the FBI guy, Sam, and his dreamy cousin, Alden. We knew what the guys who had kidnapped Carly looked like, but probably not most of their real names. We had a sketchy idea about where they'd kept her, but it had already been checked out by SWAT and had been wiped clean. We knew Bobby buff was involved because he had access to Carly's house and the others referred to him in a way that made it sound like he was in charge of them. We knew they'd been using Carly's car that was probably supposed to be her graduation present. And we guessed that her parents' estate lawyer could be in on it. And maybe Mr. Wiske, the gym teacher, who had kept her phone so she couldn't contact anyone. And probably some of the policemen. We just didn't know who. And we knew Mike had sent me the letters every month telling me not to say anything about Carly as a way—and this was our best and admittedly generous guess—to help me remember what happened and push me to do something.

We also knew that there was something about The Flower Cart Bobby buff wanted to know—probably where the money was hidden, but maybe something else, too—and that he'd taken the list when he'd knocked me out with drugs at The Flower Cart. And, of course, the money. We knew there was a lot of it hidden under the flower cooler at The Flower Cart but were divided in our discussions over whether Trudy Tilden knew about it. We didn't know who had been chasing Jess and me the day we left for Sarasota, though we still high fived each other every time the matter came up. We didn't know why Trudy Tilden abruptly sold me her business. We must have most of the information to figure out the mess that started at the Bagel Cafe, but it felt like a code; a code that started at the Bagel Cafe.

"I'm going to go to the Bagel Cafe and get a cherry cola. Anyone interested?" I said, looking at Jess.

Jess shook her head, "This is bad. This is bad."

She got up to get some jam for the rest of the biscuits, while Carly motioned for me to leave without her as she peered at the list.

29

I sat alone in the Bagel Cafe, eating a Bagel Burger with fries and sipping cherry cola. When I wasn't looking Jess had eaten the only biscuit I'd meant to crumble up in my soup, so I decided to think of the soup at my apartment as the first course of a two-course dinner. You're wondering how I could eat after what I'd seen? I wondered the same thing, myself. How does anyone eat or sleep after finding out terrible things about awful people? Knowledge like that should drive them into an extended fast and sleepless nights. Then again, if the wicked things of this world did that, most of the population would be thin and tired. But it's not. And here I was. I took another sip of cherry cola.

What happened the night of August 8th when I was sitting alone there while Jess was in the bathroom? What noises had I heard? I watched the servers behind the counter, listened hard with my right ear to the clatter of dishes, and thought back to the commotion at the beginning of it all. After listening and turning possibilities over in my mind, I concluded the sounds were probably just someone dropping something or hurrying to the kitchen or ducking out of sight of the threat at the cash register.

I looked in the window and tried to visualize the reflection I saw that night. What if my creepy thoughts weren't creepy at all, but were on target? Maybe Mr. Baxtrom's death was a hoax, and he somehow stayed out of sight or lived somewhere else. Not every conjecture is wrong just because you don't have proof. Not every suspicion is wrong just because it scares you. If that was the case, the ghost I'd seen and didn't want to admit I'd seen since it was too spine-chilling to think about wasn't a ghost at all.

But why in the world would Mr. Baxtrom want everyone to think he was dead? Was he tired of his marriage and avoiding divorce and the hassles that went with it? I gave it a minute's thought, but I didn't think so. A man who had flowers sent to his wife every week whether or not he was dead or alive wasn't someone in the market for divorce. So he wanted everyone, wife or not, to think he was dead. What kind of a weird, perverted, psycho person does that? I mean besides the people who are into zombies, but that's beside the point.

I took another sip from my glass and jumped when I felt a presence to my left. If not for my ear being dead, I probably would've heard it, too, but I didn't. I looked up right into the chocolaty brown eyes of hunky Kent Damon of the FBI.

"May I?" he asked as he slid into the seat across from me.

Could the guy ever look ordinary like the rest of us? Even in a t-shirt and jeans he was one beautiful man. I looked up at the ceiling, trying to clear my thoughts. I wished I could look at him forever, but not just now when I was trying to figure out something that he was trying to figure out too, but might think I was part of if he looked closely enough. I looked across the table and caught him looking up to where I'd been staring at the ceiling. Apparently he didn't know my looking there was his fault, not a clue to August 8th and everything that went with it.

"Let me start," he said as though we were continuing a conversation and he hadn't just sat his beautiful self down a few seconds before.

"You were followed by a Black Buick Legacy when you took that little trip in November."

I felt the blood drain from my face and grabbed the edge of the table to steady myself.

"Um, I didn't really go to Vegas," I admitted.

I started to feel guilty because he obviously had known more about that trip than he'd said when it came up at The Flower Cart.

Kent struggled against a smile that tugged the corners of his mouth. I wished I could touch it, but I ate another french fry instead to calm myself.

"I was in that car," Kent said. "Noah was driving or we wouldn't have lost you. That was quite a trick you pulled. I'm impressed."

I tried very hard to think of something to say; something intelligent and funny and flirty.

"Um, I didn't really go to Vegas."

Kent nodded.

"Wait. What? *You* were in the car that was chasing us?"

It had taken a few minutes for it to register, but I mentally patted myself on the back for catching up.

"So where exactly was it you were going?"

He raised his eyebrows as he asked the question. I sighed while Kent signaled the waitress to refill my cherry cola and ordered a coffee. Oh, sure. He ordered a coffee. He probably took it black. His drink had years of experience and sophistication over mine. It was only a matter of time before I was a goner. I'd better kick it up a notch to maintain some sense of dignity.

"Kent."

"Ah ha. You remember my name."

I couldn't believe it. He actually joked with me. My resolve to play it cool just had another three bricks knocked out of it.

"Maybe I should be asking why you were chasing us?"

Kent cleared his throat.

"I was trying to figure out what part you played in all of this. Noah had no concerns about you, but I needed to follow up."

"And what did you find?"

I wiped the palms of my hands on my jeans. Where were Carly and Jess when I needed them?

Kent tilted his head. "I'm not sure."

A look flickered over his face that made me think he wished we knew each other as more than just FBI agent and owner of The Flower Cart. Then he actually took a moment and looked into my eyes—kind of like he wanted to take a break from his FBI business and just be a guy sitting across from someone he liked. He could turn his chocolaty browns on me as long as he wanted to. I was helpless to do anything but look back.

Then he recited the Miranda warning to me. The way things were going, my jeans would have to be rung out by the end of our conversation.

"Your turn."

"My turn what?"

"I gave you information. Now you give some to me."

"Oh. Well, um, my friend, Jess, and I went down to Sarasota, Florida because I wanted to visit my old boss, Trudy Tilden. Your turn."

I could play with the best of them.

"Ah ah ah. Not so fast."

The ensuing conversation started with Kent of the godlike stature asking if we'd found my old boss and ended with me blabbing every word we said when we found her. I was doing my best, but honestly, it was all I could do to look in his eyes and not fall at his feet and offer a massage.

When I came to my senses I asked, "How did you know where to look for Carly?"

Kent squinted at me.

"You know, when SWAT went out there to find her and the place was wiped clean?"

"How did you know about that?" Kent asked, frowning.

Oh no. I'd completely forgotten I wasn't supposed to know it. To make things worse, I had used Carly's name. For all I knew he was visualizing my signed confession as he took another sip of black coffee while I grasped for something to show I wasn't the suspect I looked like.

"Oops, I forgot. My turn," I said, trying to distract from my gaffe the size of Montana.

Kent raised his sexy eyebrows at me again. Had the man no mercy?

"Well, I, um, you know how small towns are. Word gets around."

I couldn't very well roll over on Noah after he gave Kent Damon the impression there were no concerns about me. Which, let's be clear, there weren't. Plus, Noah had written me a nice little thank you note on notebook paper for helping figure out his wife's Christmas gifts and dropped it off at The Flower Cart before New Year's. That was as much class as I could ever expect from Noah. I was proud of him for thinking of writing one at all.

Kent studied me so I kept talking. I know, not the greatest idea, but I couldn't seem to help myself.

"The guys there, you know—the ones out there at the house—I s'pose it was a house just from hearsay 'n all. Anyway, they, one or two of them, probably came into town here and told someone down at the grocery mart or wherever and bam! Everyone hears about it."

"Mm hm. Whether or not it got around town as you say, some things are still classified."

"Moving on then," I hurried to extricate myself from the question I hadn't been supposed to ask. "Do you know if drugs are involved in the Bagel Cafe thing?"

I looked around The Bagel Cafe. The patrons were eating their supper like meek little lambs unaware of the conversation taking place at my table that would go down in the history of my life as one of the most worrisome, sweaty, stomach-fluttering events I'd ever experienced. Considering the last two years, that was saying a lot.

"Why do you think there are drugs involved?"

"I. Hm. I . . . was just . . . you know . . . hypothesizing."

It's wonderful when you can use science terms in real life.

Kent leaned his sinewy forearms on the table and looked directly into my eyes, past my defenses, and right into my insecurities.

"Patty, you and I both know that you have some information you aren't sharing. Now why don't we lay all the cards on the table so we can get to the bottom of this, hm? Why don't we start with the night of August 8th? Was there a reason other than being hungry that you came here that night?"

"I was here with my friend, Jess."

Kent nodded.

"We were here because our friend, Carly, had a date with Alden who is amazing and we wanted to see how it went, but we got to the theater after the movie started because we couldn't stop laughing, and it was so dark we couldn't see where they were sitting, so we came here to wait until the movie was over."

Understanding dawned on Kent Damon's face and he even looked a little sympathetic, at which point the dam burst.

"We found Carly! She's staying at my apartment until we make sure those guys aren't a threat to her anymore."

"You found Carly? The witness?"

"In Sarasota, not Vegas."

Kent looked a little like he wasn't sure whether to hug me or strangle me.

"She made a diagram of the house they kept her in. Well, actually, they kept her in a storage shed most of the time except sometimes.

"She also has a list of the names they called each other and some sketches of what they look like. Even Bobby buff. Now *there* was a surprise."

Kent began rubbing his temple.

"We didn't know he was bad. Jess had been dating him. It was only after he showed her Carly's house and told her it was going to be one of his rental properties that we figured it out.

"Don't worry, though. He doesn't know we know. He still thinks Jess likes him. She's a pretty good actress when she wants to be."

"Why didn't you come to the police with this?"

Exasperation is a word that means someone is annoyed, maybe even upset, and is in an emotional state to prove it. I would say that's where Kent was.

"We thought we'd look guilty what with Carly's name being on a car title that Gunns and Mike drove."

Kent shook his head. "Car title?"

Okay, I guess I didn't tell him everything. I added as many extras as I could think of. It isn't easy to remember everything when you're sitting across the table from someone you know you'll never again in your life be so close to and wish you could be; though he might just send you to a prison with some pretty sketchy guards because he doesn't believe you're innocent.

In a last ditch effort to help my case, I suggested one more thing.

"Plus I haven't seen the policeman who took my statement that first night, so what does that mean? Did I talk with someone who wasn't who he said he was? Or if he is a policeman, maybe he covered for the criminals. What I'm saying is . . . dirty cops? How could we trust anyone?"

Kent signaled the waitress for the check. He paid for mine. I nearly wept from delight.

"Patty,"

My name on his lips. I was beyond helpless.

"I'd like to stop at your shop if it's okay with you."

I nodded. We got to my car and I tripped as I was getting in. He caught me before I fell.

30

My hand shook as I unlocked the door to The Flower Cart. The familiar musky, floral scent drifted toward us and sedated me somewhat, which was good. Not like drugs. I don't do drugs. More like hot cocoa on a snow day when you were going to have a math test, but school was called off due to poor road conditions. I flipped on the light, let him look in every nook and cranny, and then unscrewed the grill of the flower cooler. Kent shined his flashlight on the bags and let out a low whistle. I'm pretty sure it wasn't because of my vacuuming skills.

He made some phone calls and looked out the front window of my shop.

A few police cars showed up and Noah, who was in one of them, took charge of moving the bags. I can't explain it, but

I was kinda proud of him. I think he was, too. Kent assured me SWAT was descending on the Baxtrom estate and rescuing anyone they found there. We drank some coffee while waiting in my office.

"Do you need to go to the Baxtrom house?" I asked.

Kent slowly shook his head.

"Do they need you out in front?" I pointed to where bank bags were piling up like a midwinter snowstorm.

Kent sighed. "I told them I'm staying with an important witness."

Then he smiled at me and I smiled back.

It seemed completely normal on an otherwise anything but normal day. But something was bothering me about the money. How could Trudy—if that's who had hidden it—have managed to get it all to The Flower Cart in the first place?

Kent must have been thinking along the same lines because we both looked at each other at the same time and said, "The delivery truck". It was poetry. I pulled the key from my desk drawer and we went out the back way.

Strange. A car I hadn't seen in a couple of years was parked next to the truck, and its owner was arguing with someone in the passenger seat. I walked over and peered through the window, knocking on the glass. Trudy Tilden looked back at me, screwed her mouth to one side, and nervously got out. Her passenger looked at me, and I looked at him with all kinds of unspoken questions. Francis stayed in the car. My guess was that he was hoping he was invisible. Join the club.

I rubbed my eyes, but it didn't make my former boss go away. She was there in the flesh, though I still struggled with seeing her as a bleached blonde.

"Ms. Tilden?"

"And who is this?" Trudy asked looking suspiciously at Kent Damon.

"This is Kent, a . . . um. . . a friend of mine."

He was so not a friend, though I wished heart and soul he was that and more. I just didn't know what side to play at the moment. Having Kent Damon, Francis, and Trudy Tilden in The Flower Cart parking lot at all, much less at the same time, was more than I knew what to do with.

I held my breath, hoping Kent Damon would tone down his FBI persona so Trudy wouldn't become skittish. Trudy frowned at him and pressed her lips together.

"Forgive me for surprising you like this, Patty. I stopped to see if you were in the shop, but all of the commotion in front unsettled me. So I drove around back instead."

I didn't ask her if she'd forgotten the store hours—unlikely. My suspicions were growing, but I kept my mouth shut.

"This conversation is private," Trudy added, looking sharply at Kent.

Kent walked closer and, from the change of Trudy Tilden's expression, his molten brown eyes must have had the same effect on her as on yours truly.

"Ms. Tilden, my name is Kent Damon. I'm with the FBI. I'm sorry to have surprised you like this. It was unintentional.

But I really do want to help sort things out with The Bagel Cafe incident as well as a few other things. That's why I came back to Patty's flower business with her. Since you were the previous owner, I need to advise you of your rights before you say anything else."

I held up my hand, and Mr. brown eyes actually stopped what he was saying.

I walked around to the passenger side of Trudy's car and motioned for Francis to get out. After all, hearing Kent recite what he must know as well as I knew Mrs. Baxtrom's garden club and flower show planning committee orders was fine 'n all, but once in one night was enough and three times might just send me over the edge.

Then Kent proceeded to recite the same thing to Trudy and Francis as he had to me.

It's interesting, isn't it, that everyone is so concerned about the bad guys not confessing their sins in case they just might have consequences. The whole thing came about when the lawyer of a guy by the name of Ernesto Miranda, had his conviction overturned because he said Ernesto didn't understand that he could keep his mouth shut instead of admitting he was a rapist and burglar and so on and so forth. It's okay, though. Ernesto was killed in a bar fight thirteen years later and the guy that killed him used *his* Miranda rights to not admit it and escape to Mexico. The law should have something that says 'Be sure your sins will find you out', but it doesn't.

Trudy Tilden paused.

"There's no going back, Ms. Tilden. It's best to clear the air and I'll see what I can do for everyone involved."

Trudy Tilden rubbed her nose.

"Oh all *right,*" she said rather perturbed. "You can listen in, but I didn't come to you, young man. I came to talk to Patty. If you need to talk with me after this, fine; but first I'm going to say what I came to say."

"Yes Ma'am."

Trudy Tilden's long, drawn-out sigh seemed to hold years of discouragement, fear, and frustration.

"You see, Patty, when you came to visit me in Sarasota and implied I'd been hiding, you were right. I *had* been and felt quite upset and exposed when you found me. I've since moved out of that residence. I'll have to find another," she added under her breath, smoothing her hair with a trembling hand.

Sighing again, she continued, "Let me start at the beginning. Do you remember the flower cart I used to push around town, selling flowers?"

I nodded.

"I had never thought of opening a shop. I couldn't afford it! But someone came to me and offered to pay a rather large down payment on the store, and I thought my ship had come in."

"Was it Mr. Baxtrom?"

I had to ask.

Trudy Tilden nodded, looking a little surprised.

"The very same. I signed the papers and moved my business to the building you still have today. He even offered to provide a refrigerated flower truck and deliver flowers for me, which would have been a major start-up expense. It was like manna from heaven. I didn't know why he would be so generous, and I didn't care. I just wanted to be glad for it.

"But as time went on, I started noticing a few things. First of all, there were standing orders to certain people which, I guess if you have the money, is common enough; although in a town this size it was surprising. But it seemed to me that the orders filled up the truck more quickly than I would have thought, knowing how many left the store."

I squinted, trying to figure out what exactly that meant. Was she saying he added to the orders? Who adds more flowers to a flower delivery truck? It was probably five yards tops from the door to the delivery truck whether it was parked in front or back. There wasn't anything but air and blacktop in between.

"Oh yes," Trudy hurried on. "I checked the delivery truck from time to time because I was intent on watching my pennies. It was a habit.

"Then one day when Baxtrom left on his lunch break, I climbed into the truck to check on the arrangements. I stooped to pick up a stray slip of paper and written on it was an address in Miami!"

"Florida?"

"Florida! I recalled that he had asked to use the truck to haul some new furniture down to his vacation home in Key Biscayne. Of course I'd said yes at the time. After all, he'd done so much to help me, and though the truck was in my name, he'd supplied the money to buy it. I'm not much for geography. I just figured he'd made a stop in Miami on his way there or back.

"But as I stood in the middle of the truck thinking all of this over, it occurred to me that the inside was smaller than it looked from the outside. After knocking some things around, I found false sides and a false back. Behind the false back I found packages underneath some bricks of floral foam. I pulled one out and brought it into the back office.

"I . . ." Trudy stopped abruptly and examined her fingernails for a moment.

"Well, I won't go into every detail other than to say that my benefactor who offered to deliver flowers was actually using my shop, *my shop* as a front for drug deliveries!"

"Among other things," I muttered under my breath.

Francis was fidgeting.

I turned to him and raised my eyebrows.

"Patti, I know nothing. And I love my little daughter. That's all I gotta say."

He started swaying back and forth. I didn't blame him. Three of the four of us probably wished we could just sit in a rocking chair and self-soothe the evening away.

"I had the evidence and told Baxtrom I was going to the police," Trudy continued.

"After he left, I discovered he'd taken the package I'd retrieved from the truck, and he'd taken the truck as well. It didn't deter me, though. I was going to tell the police what I'd found even though there wasn't any evidence of the package anymore. And I did. But nothing happened.

"Then what do you know, but he died! I should have been sorry, because he really had helped me get the store and had helped business grow with deliveries, but I was just relieved.

"And his poor wife who was still grieving was thoughtful enough to suggest hiring a fellow named Robert Simpson, who had just moved here."

I gasped.

"What?" Trudy asked.

"Um, my friend dated him for awhile. He still thinks they're together, but Jess broke up with him because of some things we found out about him. But he . . . doesn't know it."

Kent Damon pulled out a notebook and started jotting down some notes.

"Oh that poor girl."

"Go on," I said, patting Trudy's arm.

"Well I interviewed him, but I didn't really care for him. Don't tell your friend."

"Instead, I found Francis, who turned out to be a godsend. When I checked the truck after he started, the interior looked more the size it should be, so I was satisfied that Mr. Baxtrom's deceitful efforts had died with him."

"And he had flowers sent to his wife every week after he died," I said softly.

"Yes," Trudy nodded. "It was in the will. It didn't make sense that such a conniving man would have such a soft spot, but apparently he did."

Kent stifled a laugh.

"But what made you sell the place so fast then?" I asked.

Trudy shook her head.

"It was a letter . . . well let me back up.

"One day your friend was standing around waiting until you had some free time to talk with her, and I noticed Mrs. Baxtrom glaring at her while she talked to someone on her cell phone. Your friend seemed totally unaware of it, but it made me nervous, considering the funny stuff that had gone on. I hated to think that *Mrs.* Baxtrom might be involved. After all, she was the treasurer . . ." Trudy Tilden's voice drifted off for a moment as she thought of something. She cleared her throat.

"The treasurer of the local garden club. Then the thing happened at the Bagel Cafe and I put two and two together. At least in *my* mind they were connected, though nothing was in the news.

"One day shortly after you'd moved back to town, Patty, I got a letter in the mail telling me that I should keep my mouth shut about what I'd found in the delivery truck or something bad would happen to me.

"I didn't know what to do because what I thought was in the past had reared its ugly head again, and I didn't know where the threat was coming from. The letter was so threatening that I was worried if I told Noah Berkl about it, I wouldn't live to see another day. So I kept my mouth shut.

"Maybe I drew the wrong conclusion about what happened at the Bagel Cafe, but I didn't want the same thing to happen to me.

"I'm sorry, but I was a coward. I took the easy way out and sold you the property that started as a dream come true, but had become a living nightmare.

"Anyway," Trudy Tilden extended her hand to me, "I came to apologize. A person might be able to hide from criminals, but there are some things she can't hide from—her own conscience, for one. I'm sorry I sold you The Flower Cart and I'm sorry you ended up carrying the load that I should've carried. I'm here," she turned to Kent Damon, "to wipe the slate clean. Only," she cleared her throat, "being here puts me in a bad spot. I'd rather leave and leave quickly than stay and put myself in more danger."

"You were brave to come, Trudy."

I grabbed her hand and pulled her into a hug.

"What about the money under the flower cooler?" I whispered.

Trudy Tilden slapped her hand over her mouth and started laughing so hard she had to lean against her car.

"You found it!" Trudy exclaimed.

I wasn't sure if she was glad or not.

"Don't think for a minute, young man, I'm hiding anything," she said to the FBI agent whose life was spent accusing people of hiding things. Of course he was thinking it.

"It's hard for an old woman to remember everything, especially when trying to get it all out in the open at the same time. Yes. The money."

Kent was all ears.

Trudy sighed again. Whether she'd planned to recover the money while she was in town or whether she had truly forgotten to mention it was a moot point. It was out of the bag now, so to speak.

You know what I think? I think 'moot' shouldn't be used as much as it is, but every once in awhile it has a place. Mr. Tyson, a college professor of Jess's used that word more than necessary. Moot means you can discuss it 'til the cows come home, but the conclusion won't make much of a difference. Jess kept saying 'moo' and I kept correcting her. It was kind of a moot point with us, too.

"When I took the package—it was a brick-like package that I assumed was drugs. I may be old, and some people might not think much of me, but I wasn't born yesterday," she said parenthetically. "And I know my plants. Cannabis has a distinct odor. Anyway, there were bags behind the false sides of the truck. Many, many green bags."

I nodded. "Bank bags."

"Yes."

"I took some of them!" Trudy put her hands over her mouth like she couldn't believe she'd said it. "Actually, I took quite a few. I still don't know how I worked up the nerve. I did not, however, show them to Mr. Baxtrom, since I was so upset about the drugs and I thought he could just jolly well worry over the money and get an ulcer.

"I kept them in various places around the shop, and just before I left I shoved them under the flower cooler. I'm sorry," she added, "It probably reduced the cooling power."

"That's okay. I vacuumed."

Kent pinched the bridge of his nose.

31

I was sitting in my office at the back of The Flower Cart doing the books. When news of the biggest drug bust and major federal investigation in this town hit the papers, it was all I could do to keep the flower cooler stocked. I even ordered extra little statuettes, bird baths and the like, and those sold like hotcakes, too. Everyone wanted a piece of the place that was part of the story. In fact, a year later business is still brisk, I've learned that working harder than you prefer has its own rewards, and I have just one more payment before this little shop is mine free and clear.

It seems that when little nobody Trudy Tilden had caught on to Mr. Baxtrom, things got too hot for the drug and sex trafficking business he'd run for years. He'd imported drugs and children to our little non-descript part of the world and sold them to dealers, perverts, and the like. It was why he was so wealthy. He talked his dear wife into reporting his death to the media, forged death certificates, and had flowers delivered weekly to keep her happy with the new arrangement. She could stay at their vacation home with him as much as she pleased, but she preferred the life she'd carved out in our small town. Go figure.

However, Mr. Baxtrom didn't trust his lovely accomplice of a wife with the dirty side of the family business. So he decided to send his nephew from their warehouse in Miami to take his place running things while he got out of town and out of the heat caused by Trudy Tilden's discovery. He moved down to his vacation home in Key Biscayne, which was closer to Miami anyway.

He kept the business running like a top by moving 'product' out of the Baxtrom estate. After I bought the business, they just picked up where they left off, and no one, meaning me, was the wiser. It was put in the back of the flower delivery truck every time Francis went into the house with Mrs. Baxtrom's flowers. When Francis parked the truck in The Flower Cart parking lot for the night, the boxes were off loaded by Gunns, Mike, Dickie, and Gemini, and redistributed to dealers by Baxtrom's nephew, Bobby buff.

It looked touch and go for Francis for awhile, but in the end there wasn't any proof he knew what was going on. A lawyer talked the jury into giving him probation and 200 hours community service for a passive cover-up even though he stuck to his claim of ignorance. But it was overturned due to lack of any real evidence. My guess? I think he turned a blind eye to suspicious situations, including the whole offloading business with the flower truck. Maybe the one day he was worried over something he'd lost had to do with the list of names and the map. Maybe he'd discovered it in the back of the truck and asked about it. And when he did, he was told to keep his mouth shut or his family would be in danger. I don't know if that's what happened, but it seems like a pretty good guess. So if it did happen that way, he'd chosen protection of his family over exposing some very bad men.. I'm not saying it was the right decision, but why quibble? It's hard to find good flower delivery drivers and Francis is a gem.

The nephew, Robert Simpson, a.k.a. Bobby buff, came to town and took over, using the four low-lifes Baxtrom had used. Bobby apparently had a personal goal of expanding the business to include property management. It was his mistake to cut corners and brag to his hot girlfriend. But that wasn't until later, which was probably a good thing for Jess. Not knowing that her sweet little snookums was a criminal protected her from months of anxiety over it. It protected her from being considered an accomplice, too.

When Mrs. Baxtrom called her husband and told him she thought Carly had seen her hand the list of drug buyers to Bobby just outside The Flower Cart, Baxtrom himself came back to engineer Carly's disappearance.

Yes, I really did see Mr. Baxtrom's ghost. Only he wasn't dead. The reflection I'd thought I saw was actually Baxtrom in the flesh standing outside the window looking in. It's funny how something that scares the daylights out of you keeps you from believing it's real.

Kent Damon, FBI, made sure Carly, Jess, and I didn't stay in trouble. He even found a nice, safe, little place for Trudy Tilden to live. It's just possible Trudy had tucked some of the found money that she didn't shove under the flower cooler in a nice, safe, little place, too; but if she did, she was the only one who ever knew it. My guess? I think she felt she'd cleared her conscience plenty, but that there was no reason to compromise the retirement plan she'd acquired the day she'd found drugs in the flower delivery truck. No amount of questioning elicited one little word about such a thing.

One unsatisfactory result of the investigation was that Mike's killer was never identified. But you know what? I think that in losing his life, he gained a good reputation, at least in our eyes. Dying as an unsuccessful hero is far better than living with the reputation of the scum of the earth.

The drug dealers on the amazingly complete and revealing list that had everybody up in arms to begin with were all sentenced five to ten years by the judges who handled their cases. Mr. Baxtrom and the rest of the guys that caused such trouble for Carly just as she was trying to become an adult and live an exciting life ended up in prison. It wasn't until I testified that I realized whose handwriting had written the list. All those special requests she'd written out for flowers for the garden club meetings came suddenly flooding back. The last I heard, in exchange for walking investigators through the money laundering she'd done on behalf of her husband's criminal activity, giving up names, and turning state's evidence, Mrs. Baxtrom got a tidy little deal with a shortened sentence and longer parole.

Bobby buff sweet talked the jury into a lighter sentence, too. He sent Jess a letter from prison. In return, she ordered a black rose from me and sent him an envelope of its petals. An English playwright named William Congreve once said something like 'hell hath no fury like a woman scorned', but anyone who knew Jess knew any guy who wanted to come near her had better tell the truth, the whole truth, and nothing but the truth or he would find out what kind of fury hell really could have.

Jess will graduate early from community college next winter. Without Bobby buff around she had more time on her hands to make extra sales calls that paid for extra classes. The extra studying kept her distracted enough that she even lost a few pounds, though she still drinks cherry cola like a maniac and I keep mint ice cream topping and whipped cream stocked for her in my refrigerator.

Alden moved back from college for the summer when the whole thing broke loose and visited Carly at her house (after the three of us had thoroughly fumigated it) to apologize for the trouble. They had a lovely conversation that ended in dinner and a movie and continued interest on both sides.

* *

Melissa knocked on the door jamb of my office.

"Yes?"

"Thank you, Ms. Calico, for giving me this job during high school. I'll never forget you."

What a nice thing for her to say, especially since her last day was two weeks before.

"I came to pick up my check."

With high schoolers it's always about the money. I pulled the check out of the top drawer of my desk and handed it to her. She handed me the day's mail and a small package.

"I don't know what this is. I found it on the counter with the other mail."

I took a package from her hands.

"Thanks, Melissa. Good luck in college!" I called to her as she was already half-way out the door.

"Anything else, Patty?" Francis called through the door Melissa had opened.

"No, Francis. See you tomorrow!"

I tore off the paper that enclosed the small package Melissa had brought in and opened the box. Inside on smooth velvet was a pin in the shape of one small red rose with a 24 carat gold stem. The 2x3 card simply said, "In another lifetime . . ." KD. I was staring into space when to my left I heard the slight sound of a paperclip. I must've dropped it. As I reached to pick it up, I tucked my hair behind my ear and, for the first time in two years, heard the whisper sound of my hand on my ear.

Made in the USA
Middletown, DE
23 July 2020

12581809R00187